Disney

THE ZODIAC LEGACY

PAPERCUTZ™

Disney Graphic Novels available from PAPERCUTZ

DISNEY THE ZODIAC LEGACY

DISNEY PLANES

DISNEY X-MICKEY

DISNEY MINNIE & DAISY BFF

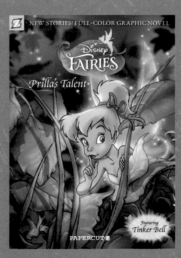

DISNEY FAIRIES #1

DISNEY FAIRIES #2

Disney graphic novels are available in paperback for $7.99 each; in hardcover for $12.99 each. Available at booksellers everywhere. Or you can order from us: Please add $4.00 for postage and handling for first book, and add $1.00 for each additional book. Please make check payable to NBM Publishing. Send to: Papercutz, 160 Broadway, Suite 700, East Wing, New York, NY 10038 or call 800-886-1223 (9-6 EST M-F) MC-Visa-Amex accepted.

#1 "Tiger Island"
Stan Lee — Creator
Stuart Moore — Writer
P.H. Marcondes — Artist

PAPERCUT Z
New York

Disney
THE ZODIAC LEGACY

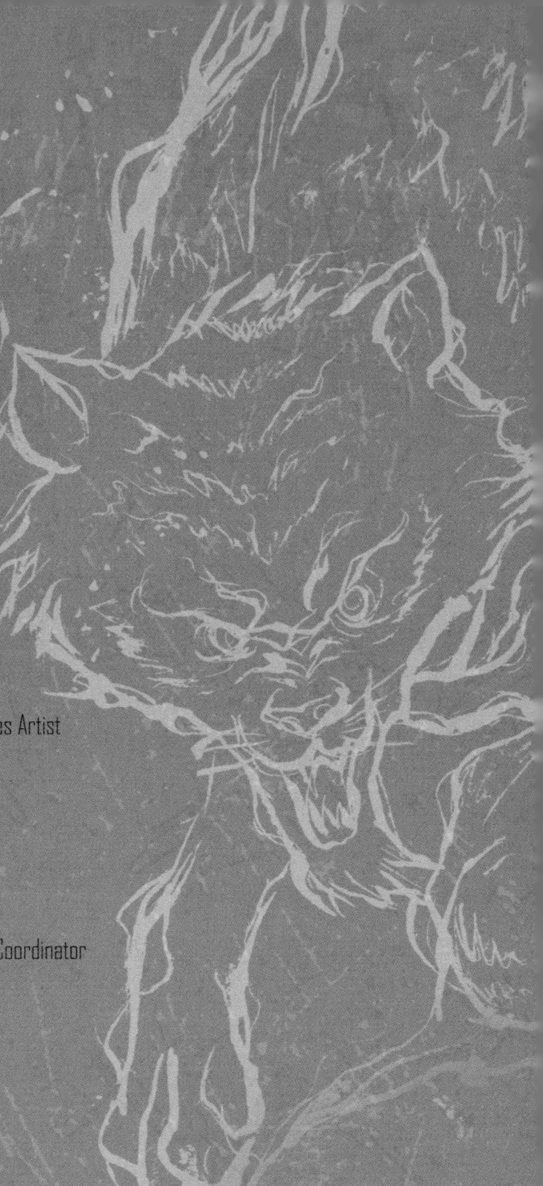

#1 "Tiger Island"
Stuart Moore – Writer
P.H. Marcondes – Artist
Andie Tong – Cover, Endpapers, and Character Profiles Artist
Jolyon Yates – Title Page Artist
Jay Jay Jackson – Character Color Design
Matteo Baldrighi – Colorist
Roberta Marchetta
Paola Selene Fiorino
Giovanni Spadaro – Color Assistants
Salvatore Di Marco (Grafimated) – Color Assistants Coordinator
Bryan Senka – Letterer
Dawn Guzzo – Production
Brittanie Black – Production Coordinator
Jeff Whitman – Assistant Managing Editor
Jim Salicrup
Editor-in-Chief

ISBN: 978-1-62991-296-7 paperback edition
ISBN: 978-1-62991-297-4 hardcover edition

Papercutz books may be purchased for business or promotional use. For information on bulk purchases please contact Macmillan Corporate and Premium Sales Department at (800) 221-7945 x5442.

Printed in Korea through Four Colour Print Group
June 2016 by WE SP Co., Ltd
79-29 Soraji-ro, Paju-Si
Gyeonggi-do, Korea 10863

Distributed by Macmillan
First Printing

The power of the Zodiac comes from twelve pools of mystical energy.

Due to a sabotaged experiment, twelve magical superpowers are unleashed on Steven Lee and twelve others.

Now Steven Lee is thrown into the middle of an epic global chase.

He'll have to master strange powers, outrun super-powered mercenaries, and unlock the secrets of the Zodiac Legacy. When Steven is first rescued by Jasmine and Carlos, he relishes his newfound powers and is excited to be on a grand adventure, alongside...

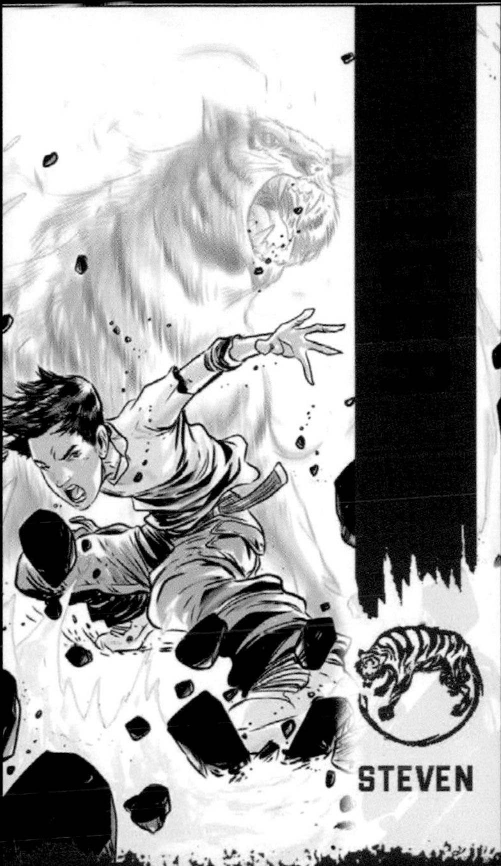
STEVEN
POWERS
STRENGTH, REFLEXES

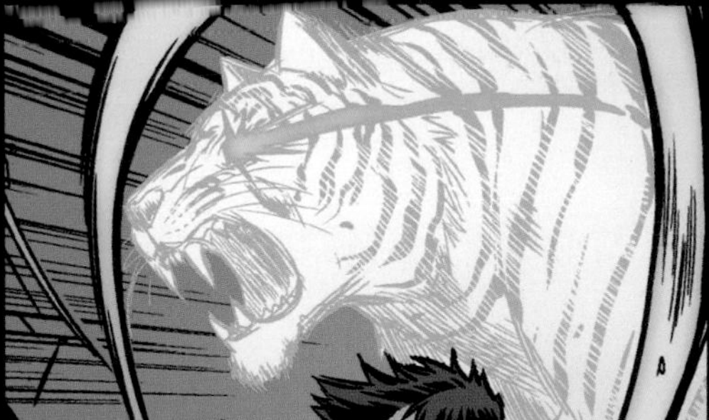

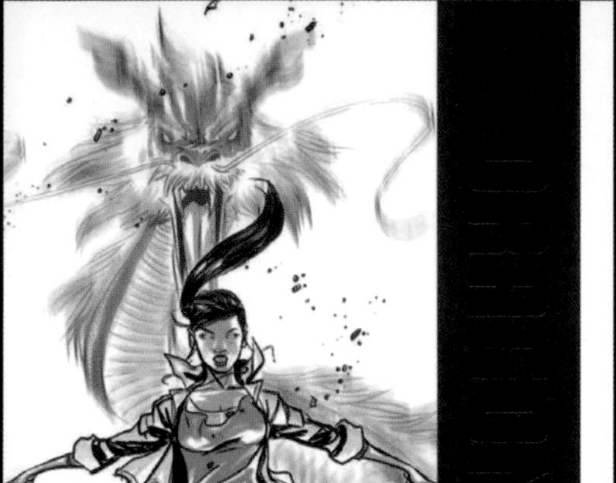
JASMINE

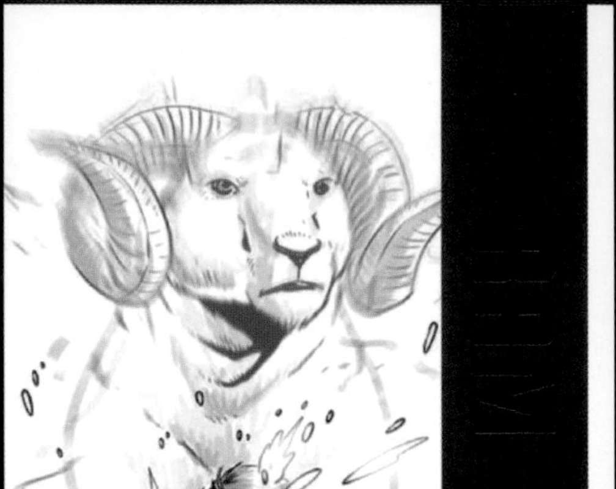
LIAM

FIRE BREATHING, FLIGHT,
MIND CONTROL

INVULNERABILITY

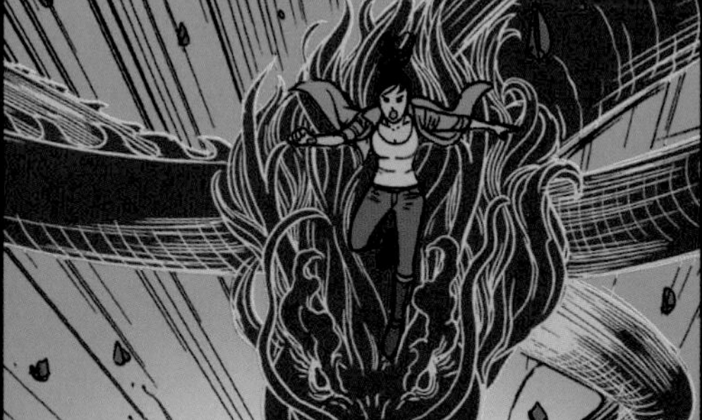

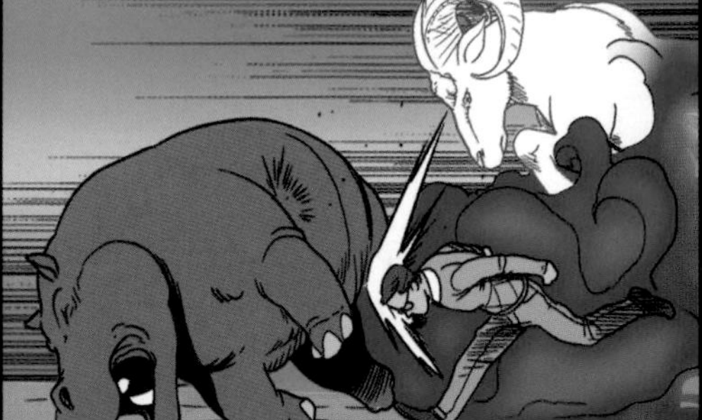

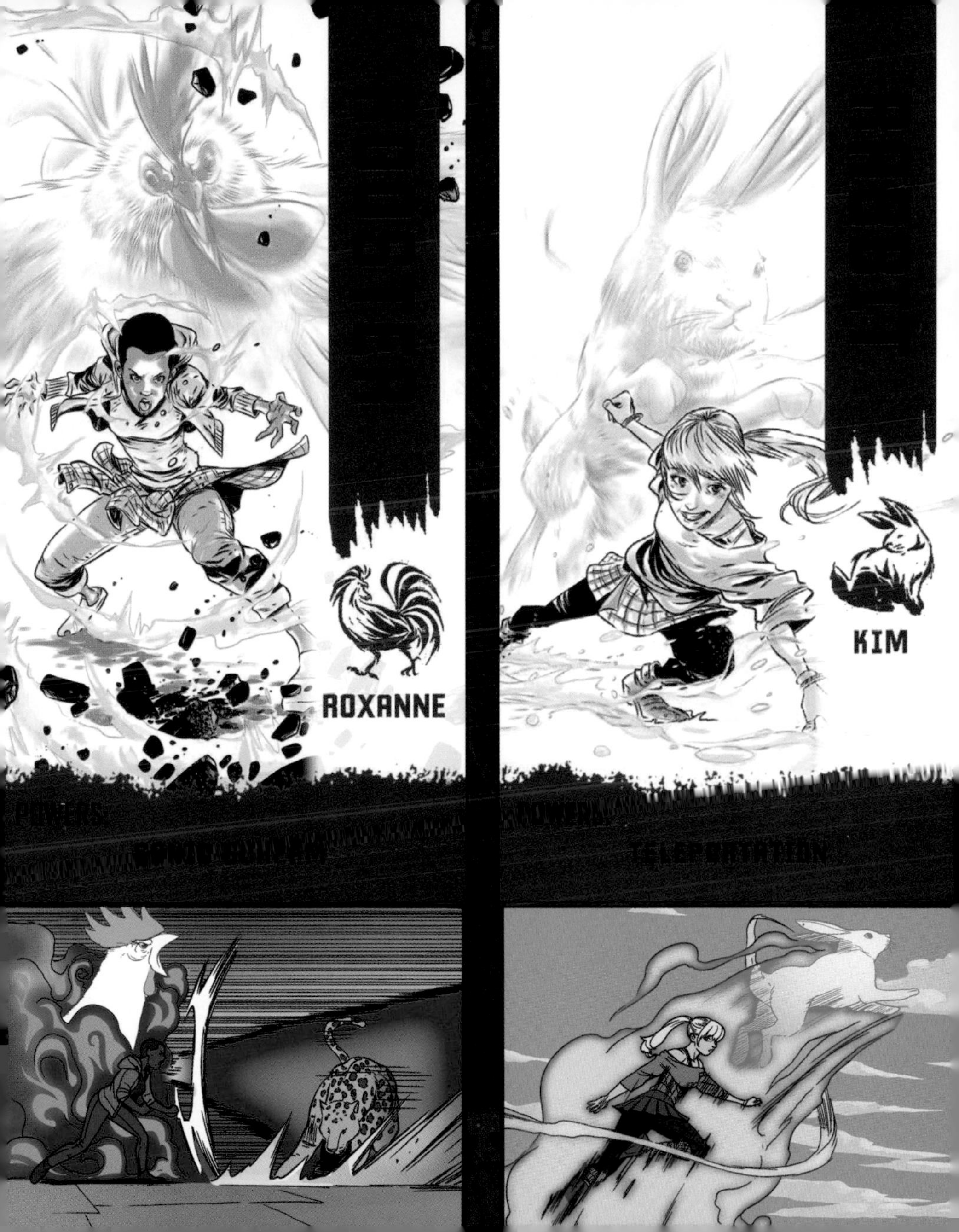
ROXANNE
POWERS:
KIM
POWERS:
TELEPORTATION

DUANE

POWERS:
INFORMATION PROCESSING

Steven and his new friends will need to stay one step ahead of the Vanguard...

DRAGON

MAXWELL

POWERS:
FIRE BREATHING, FLIGHT,
MIND CONTROL

The Vanguard
organization is
bent on tracking
down all of the
Zodiac powers.
The Vanguard are...

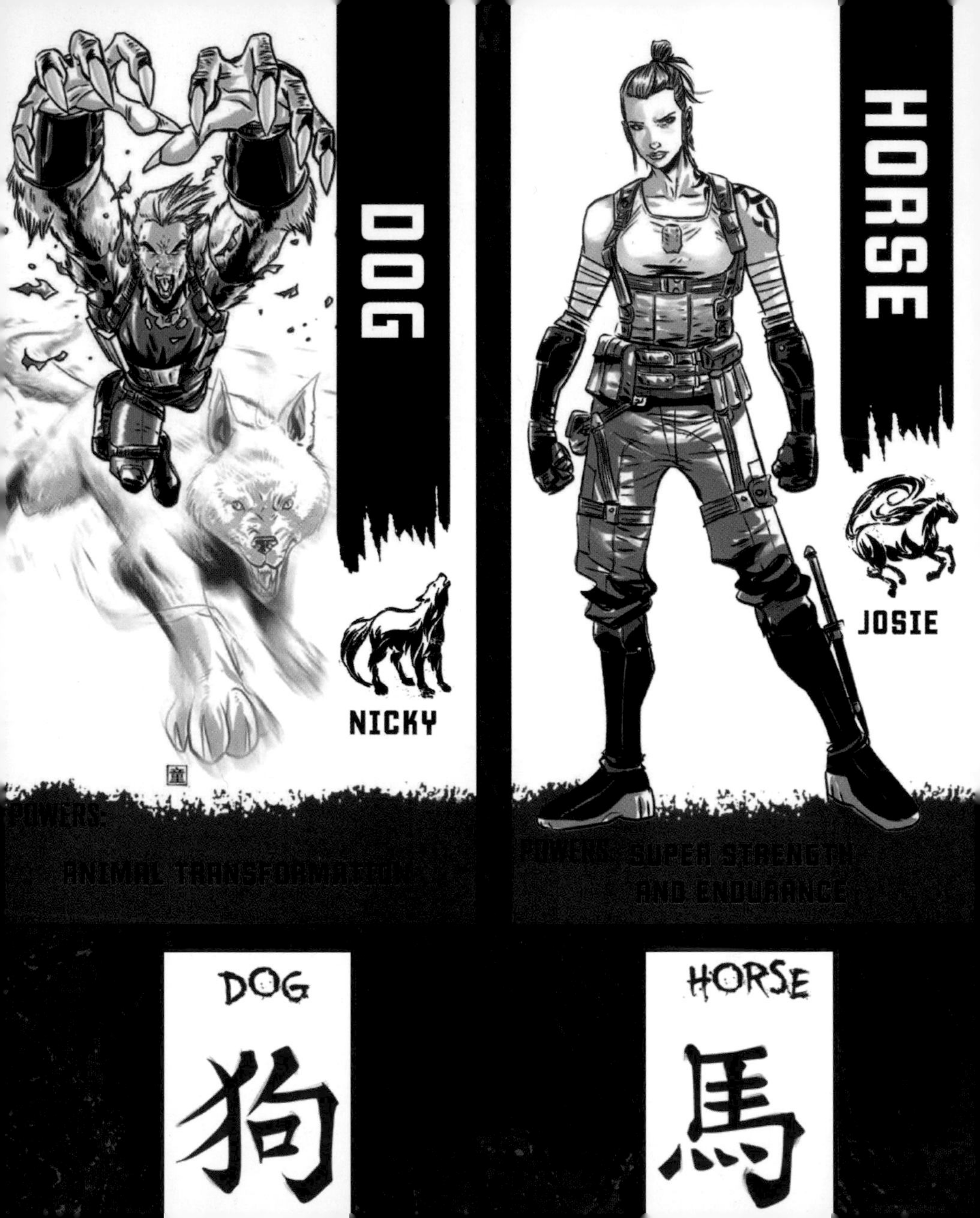

DOG
NICKY
POWERS:
ANIMAL TRANSFORMATION
DOG
狗
HORSE
JOSIE
POWERS: SUPER STRENGTH
AND ENDURANCE
HORSE
馬

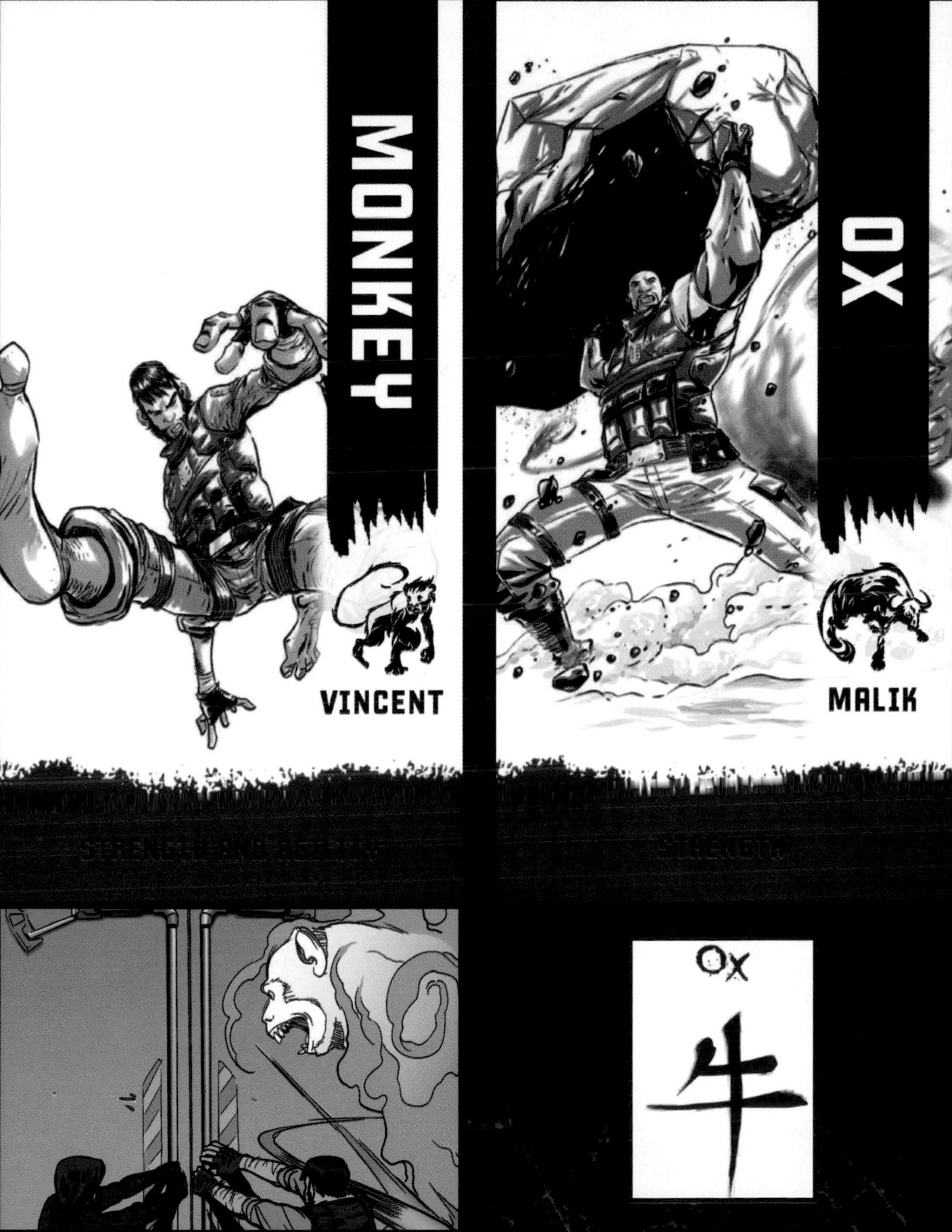
MONKEY
VINCENT
STRENGTH AND AGILITY
OX
MALIK
STRENGTH
Ox
牛

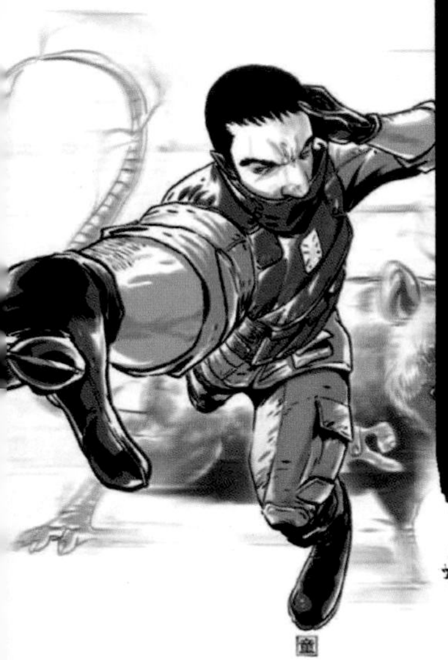

RAT

THIAGO

POWERS:
SUPERHUMAN REFLEXES
INTUITION

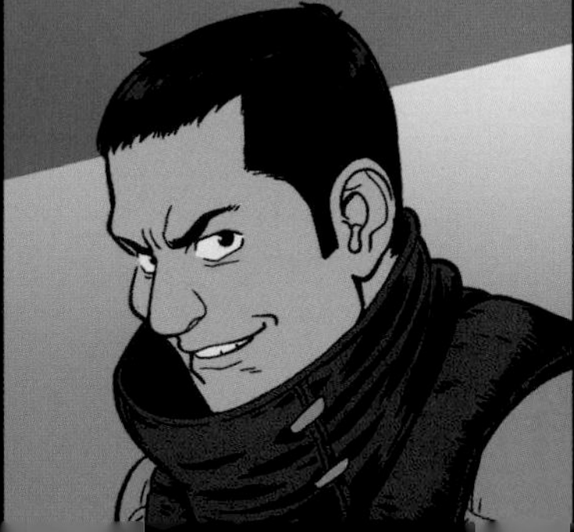

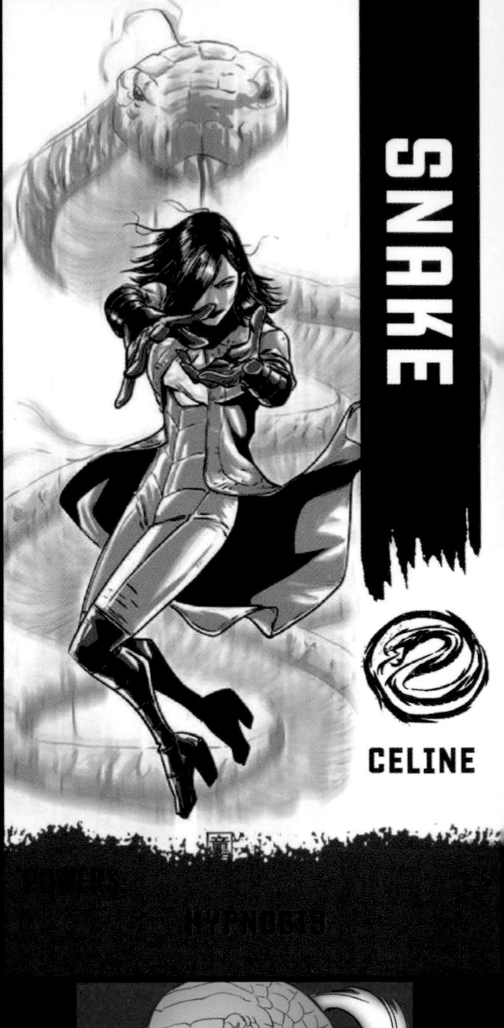

SNAKE

CELINE

POWERS:
HYPNOSIS

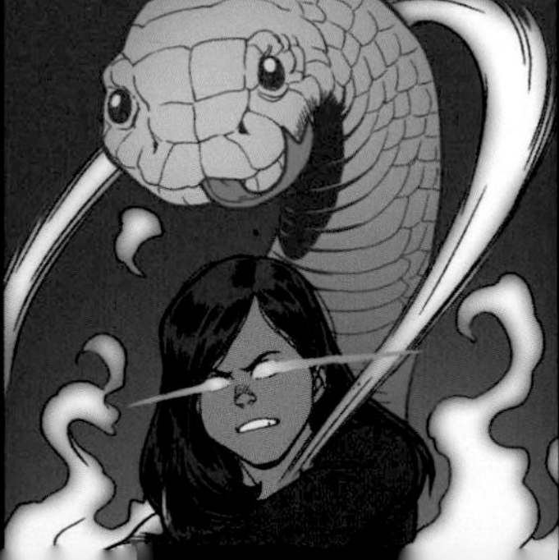

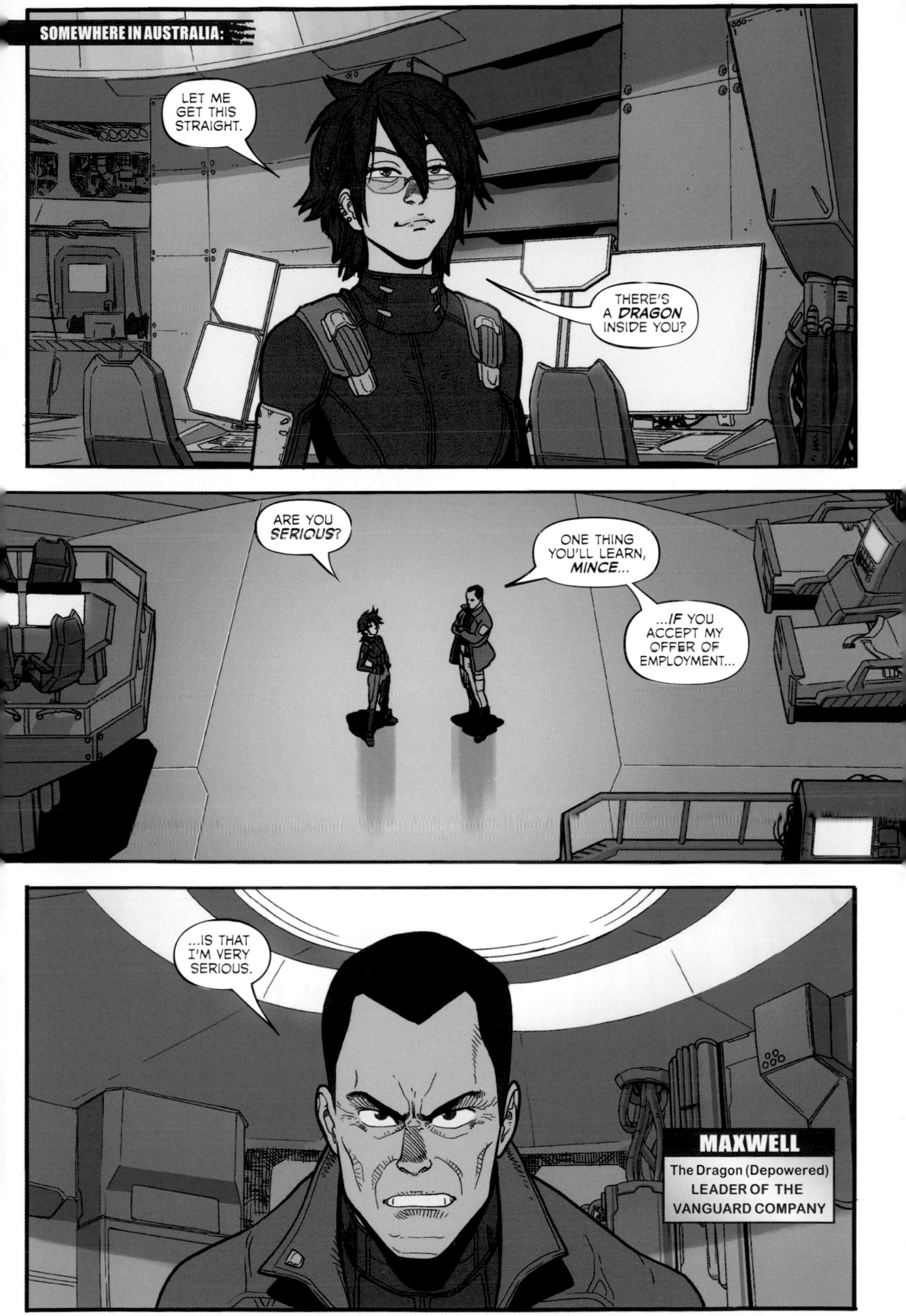
SOMEWHERE IN AUSTRALIA:
LET ME GET THIS STRAIGHT.
THERE'S A DRAGON INSIDE YOU?
ARE YOU SERIOUS?
ONE THING YOU'LL LEARN, MINCE...
...IF YOU ACCEPT MY OFFER OF EMPLOYMENT...
...IS THAT I'M VERY SERIOUS.
MAXWELL
The Dragon (Depowered)
LEADER OF THE VANGUARD COMPANY

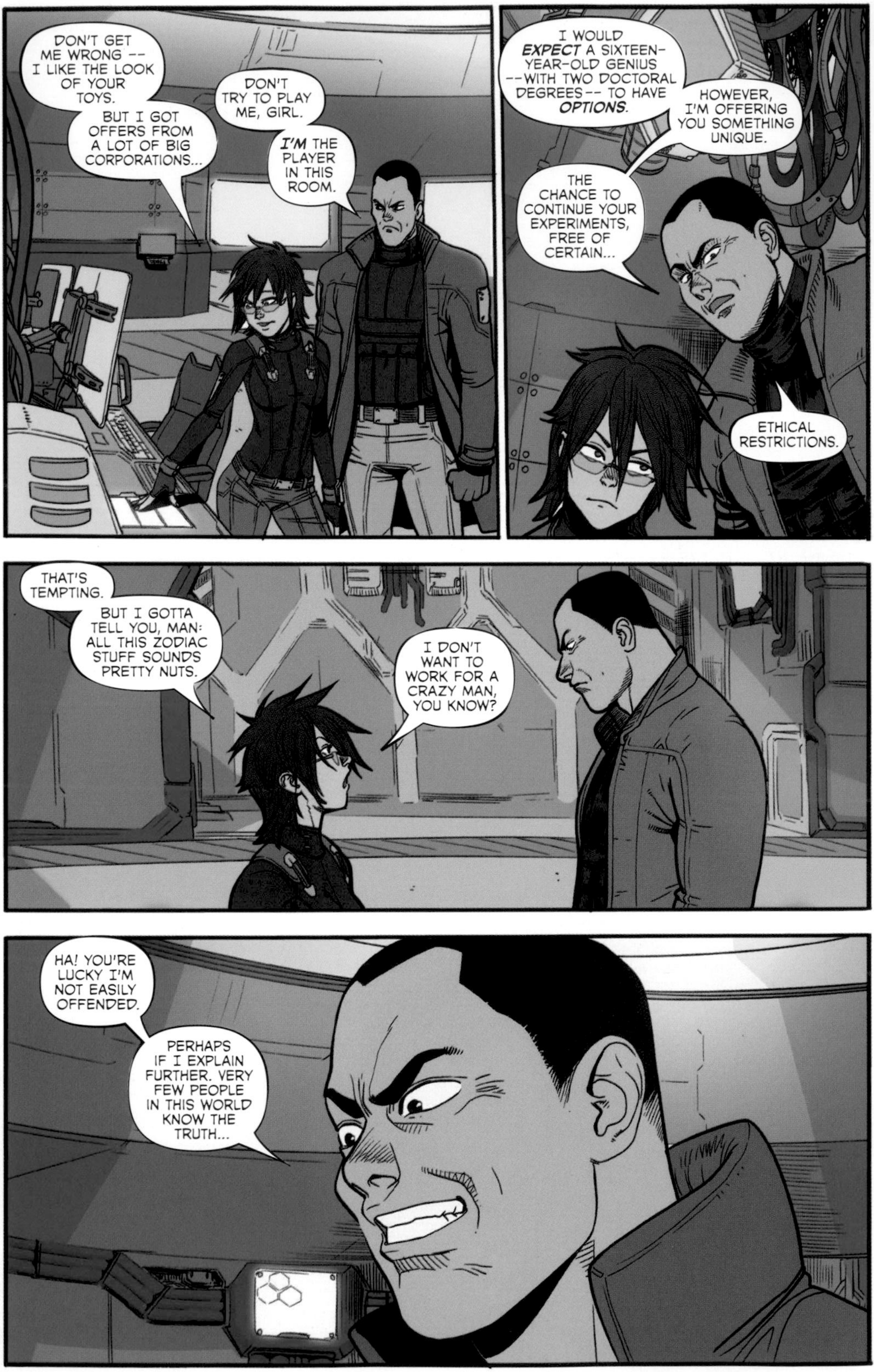
DON'T GET ME WRONG -- I LIKE THE LOOK OF YOUR TOYS.
BUT I GOT OFFERS FROM A LOT OF BIG CORPORATIONS...
DON'T TRY TO PLAY ME, GIRL.
I'M THE PLAYER IN THIS ROOM.
I WOULD **EXPECT** A SIXTEEN-YEAR-OLD GENIUS --WITH TWO DOCTORAL DEGREES-- TO HAVE **OPTIONS**.
HOWEVER, I'M OFFERING YOU SOMETHING UNIQUE.
THE CHANCE TO CONTINUE YOUR EXPERIMENTS, FREE OF CERTAIN...
ETHICAL RESTRICTIONS.
THAT'S TEMPTING.
BUT I GOTTA TELL YOU, MAN: ALL THIS ZODIAC STUFF SOUNDS PRETTY NUTS.
I DON'T WANT TO WORK FOR A CRAZY MAN, YOU KNOW?
HA! YOU'RE LUCKY I'M NOT EASILY OFFENDED.
PERHAPS IF I EXPLAIN FURTHER. VERY FEW PEOPLE IN THIS WORLD KNOW THE TRUTH...

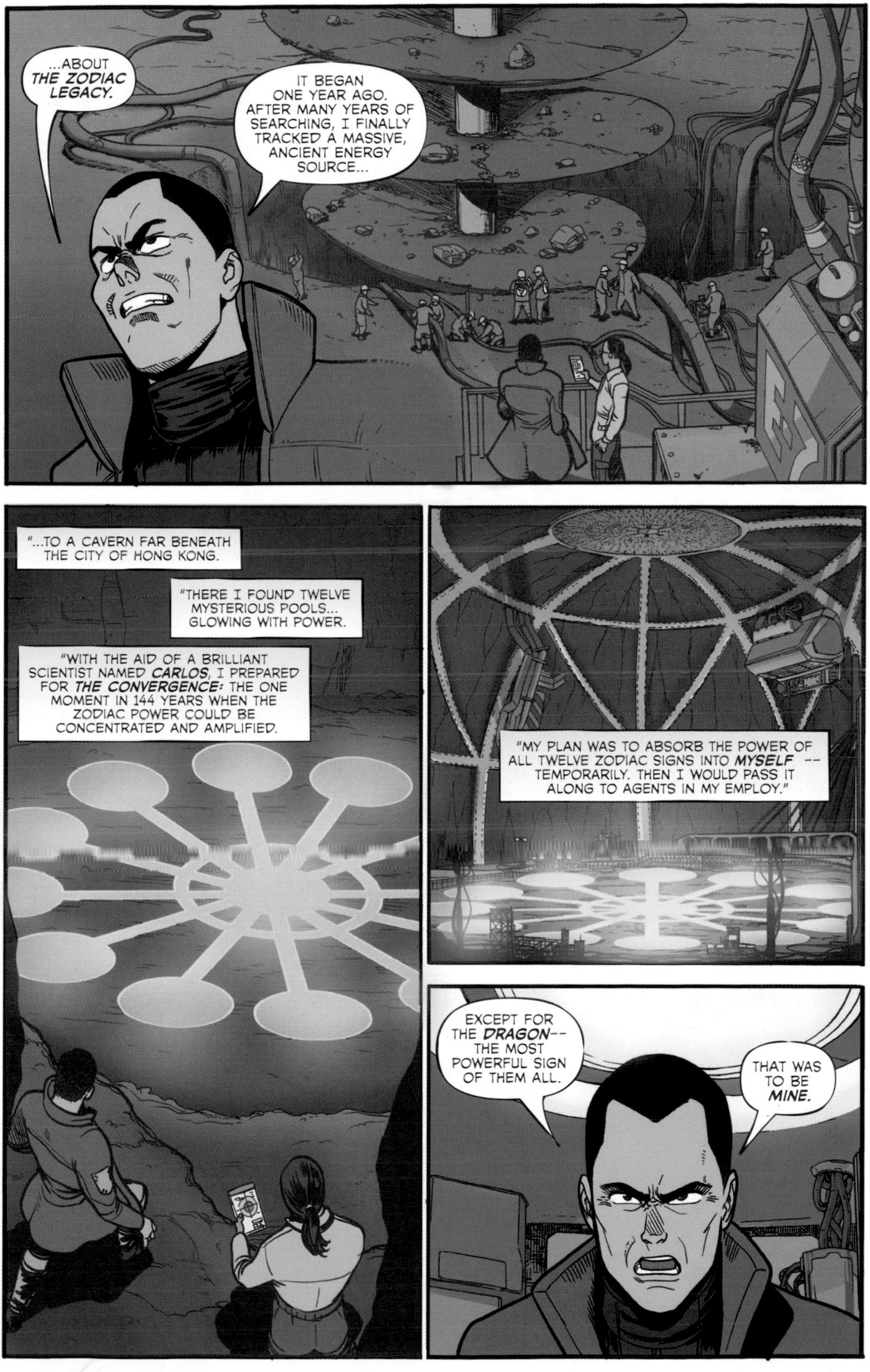
...ABOUT THE ZODIAC LEGACY.
IT BEGAN ONE YEAR AGO. AFTER MANY YEARS OF SEARCHING, I FINALLY TRACKED A MASSIVE, ANCIENT ENERGY SOURCE...
"...TO A CAVERN FAR BENEATH THE CITY OF HONG KONG.
"THERE I FOUND TWELVE MYSTERIOUS POOLS... GLOWING WITH POWER.
"WITH THE AID OF A BRILLIANT SCIENTIST NAMED CARLOS, I PREPARED FOR THE CONVERGENCE: THE ONE MOMENT IN 144 YEARS WHEN THE ZODIAC POWER COULD BE CONCENTRATED AND AMPLIFIED.
"MY PLAN WAS TO ABSORB THE POWER OF ALL TWELVE ZODIAC SIGNS INTO MYSELF -- TEMPORARILY. THEN I WOULD PASS IT ALONG TO AGENTS IN MY EMPLOY."
EXCEPT FOR THE DRAGON-- THE MOST POWERFUL SIGN OF THEM ALL.
THAT WAS TO BE MINE.

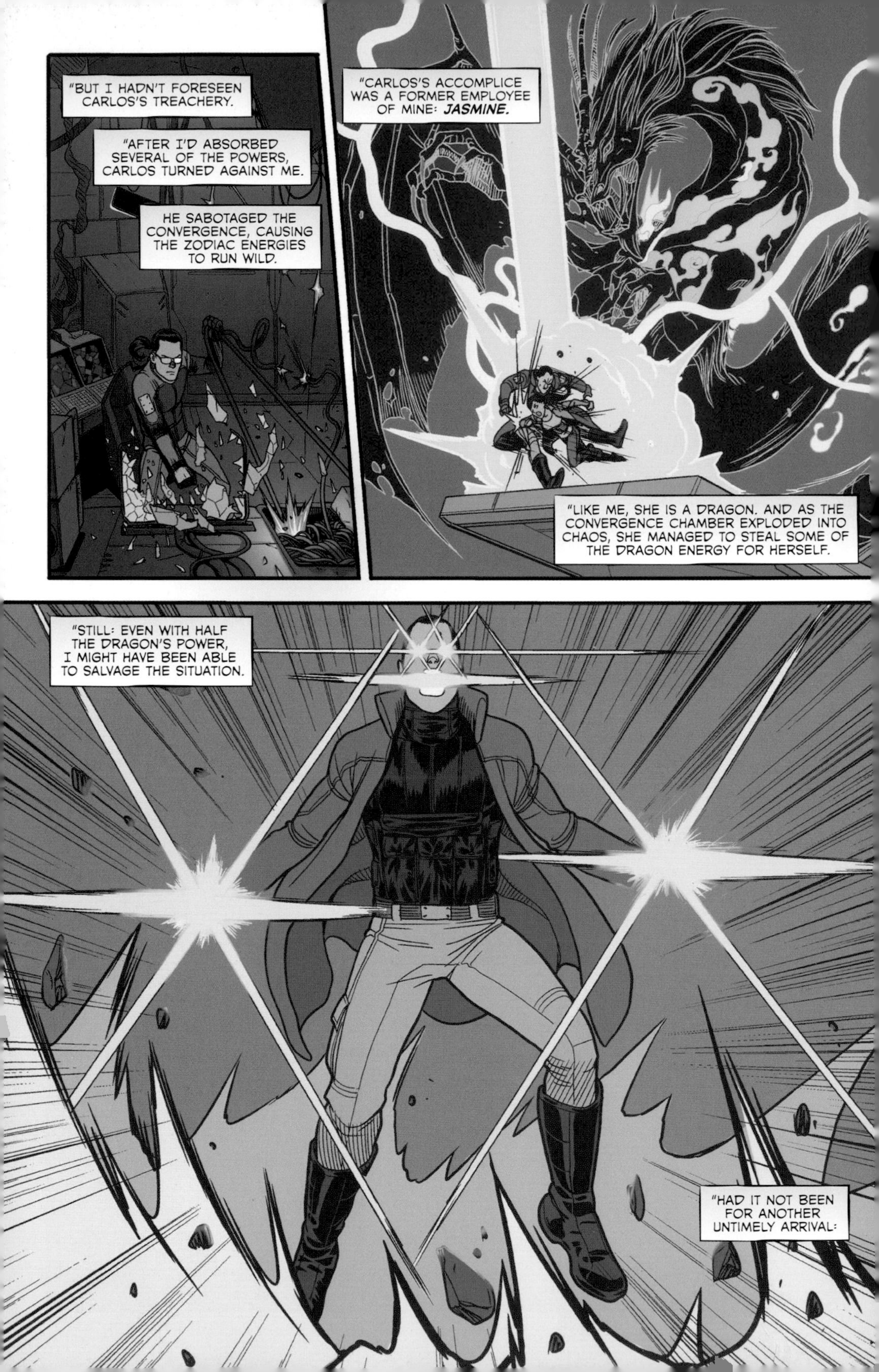
"BUT I HADN'T FORESEEN CARLOS'S TREACHERY.
"AFTER I'D ABSORBED SEVERAL OF THE POWERS, CARLOS TURNED AGAINST ME.
HE SABOTAGED THE CONVERGENCE, CAUSING THE ZODIAC ENERGIES TO RUN WILD.
"CARLOS'S ACCOMPLICE WAS A FORMER EMPLOYEE OF MINE: JASMINE.
"LIKE ME, SHE IS A DRAGON. AND AS THE CONVERGENCE CHAMBER EXPLODED INTO CHAOS, SHE MANAGED TO STEAL SOME OF THE DRAGON ENERGY FOR HERSELF.
"STILL: EVEN WITH HALF THE DRAGON'S POWER, I MIGHT HAVE BEEN ABLE TO SALVAGE THE SITUATION.
"HAD IT NOT BEEN FOR ANOTHER UNTIMELY ARRIVAL:

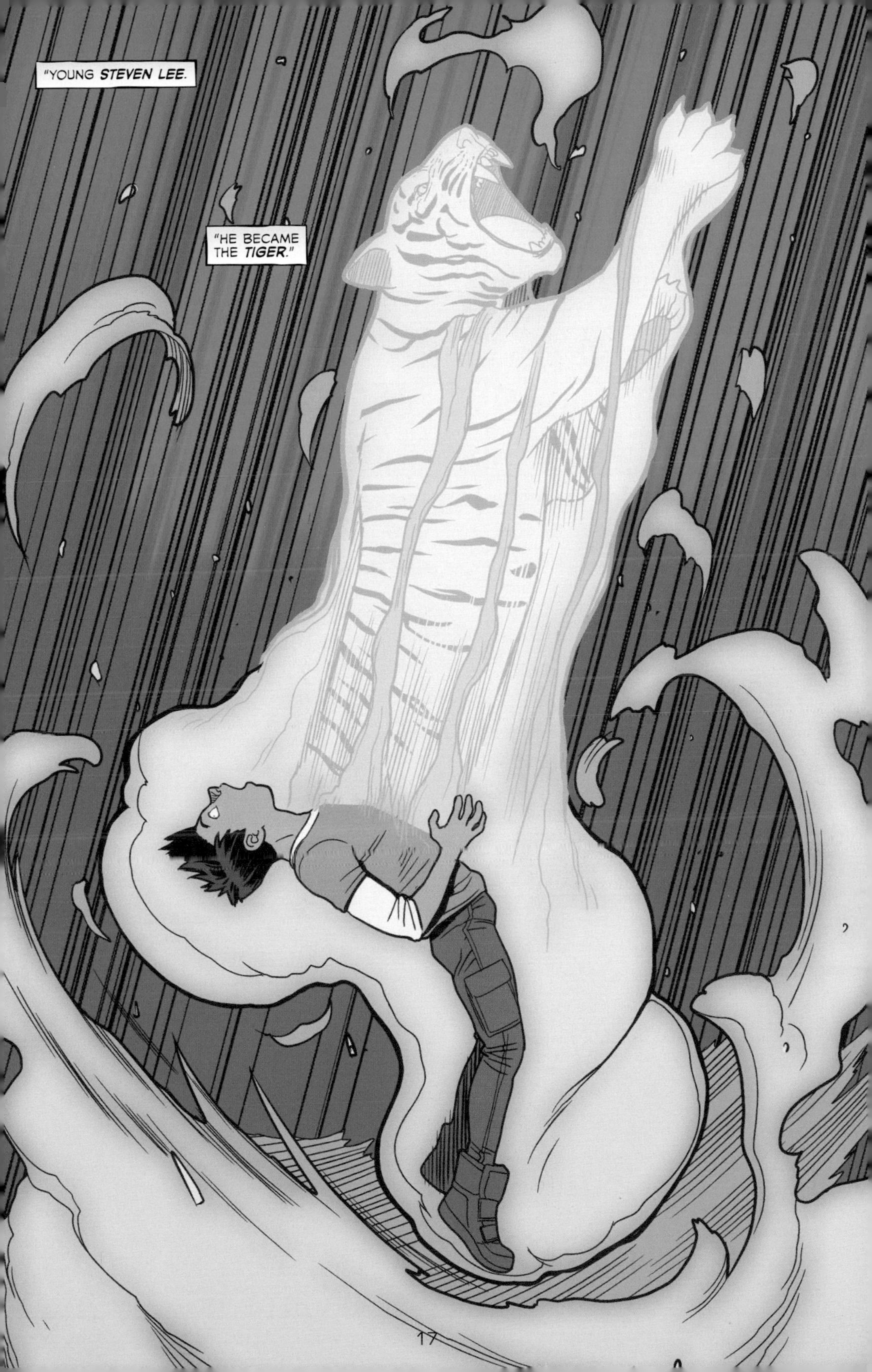
"YOUNG STEVEN LEE.
"HE BECAME THE TIGER."

SINCE THAT TIME, THE ZODIAC POWERS HAVE BEEN DIVIDED BETWEEN MY FORCES AND JASMINE'S.

BUT *YOU'RE* STILL THE DRAGON, RIGHT?

A TINY SHARD OF THE DRAGON STILL LIVES INSIDE ME. JASMINE HAS MANAGED TO SNATCH AWAY THE REST.

I INTEND TO REVERSE THAT SITUATION.

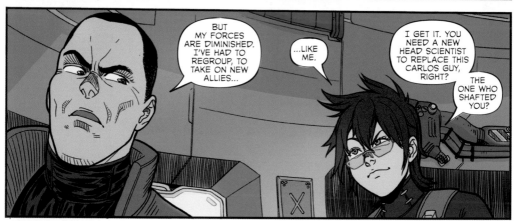

BUT MY FORCES ARE DIMINISHED. I'VE HAD TO REGROUP, TO TAKE ON NEW ALLIES...

...LIKE ME.

I GET IT. YOU NEED A NEW HEAD SCIENTIST TO REPLACE THIS CARLOS GUY, RIGHT?

THE ONE WHO SHAFTED YOU?

TAKE CARE, MINCE. WE MAY EVENTUALLY WORK WELL TOGETHER.

BUT DON'T *EVER* THINK YOU CAN OUTGUESS ME.

18

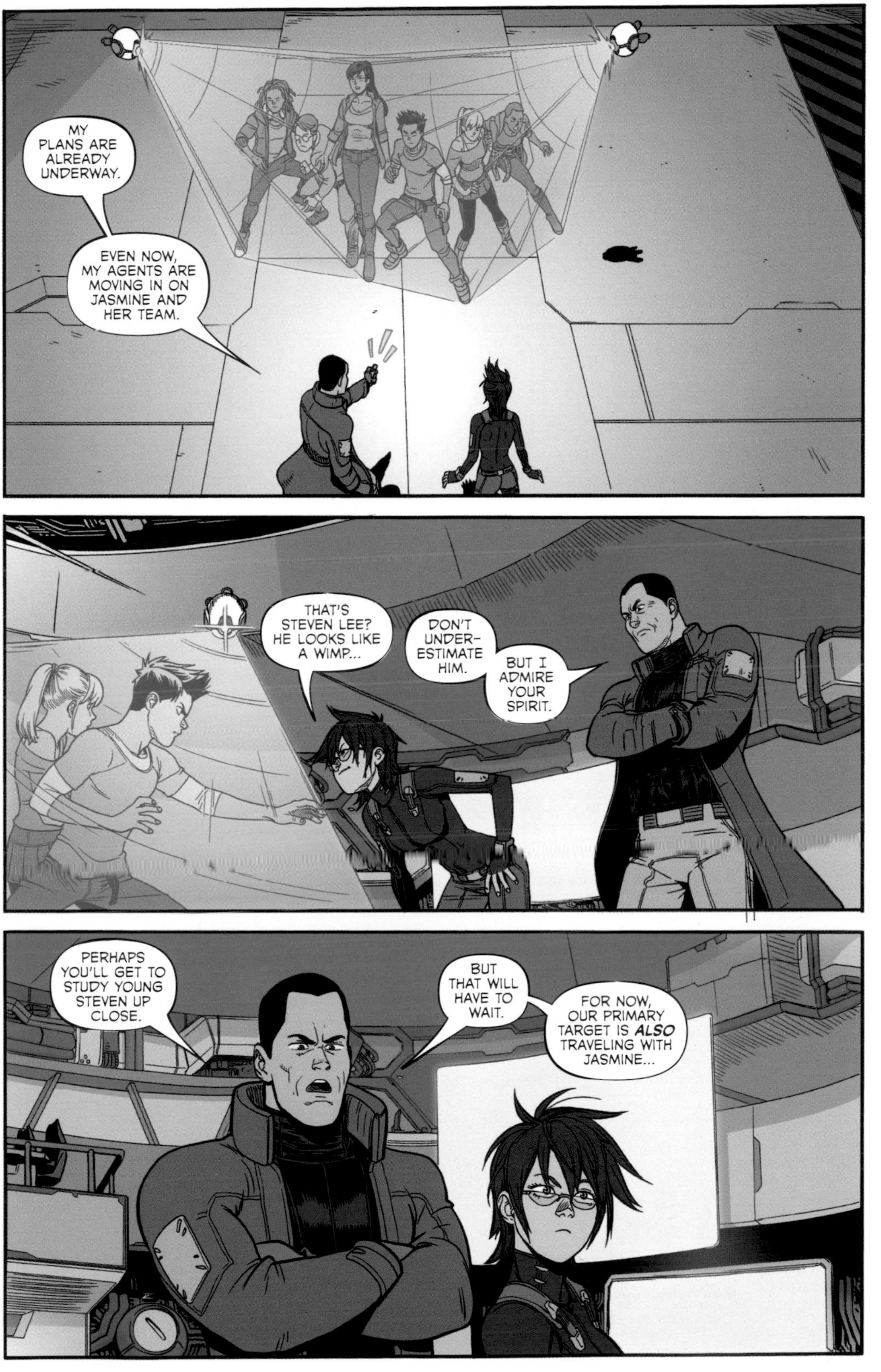
MY PLANS ARE ALREADY UNDERWAY.
EVEN NOW, MY AGENTS ARE MOVING IN ON JASMINE AND HER TEAM.
THAT'S STEVEN LEE? HE LOOKS LIKE A WIMP...
DON'T UNDER-ESTIMATE HIM.
BUT I ADMIRE YOUR SPIRIT.
PERHAPS YOU'LL GET TO STUDY YOUNG STEVEN UP CLOSE.
BUT THAT WILL HAVE TO WAIT.
FOR NOW, OUR PRIMARY TARGET IS *ALSO* TRAVELING WITH JASMINE...

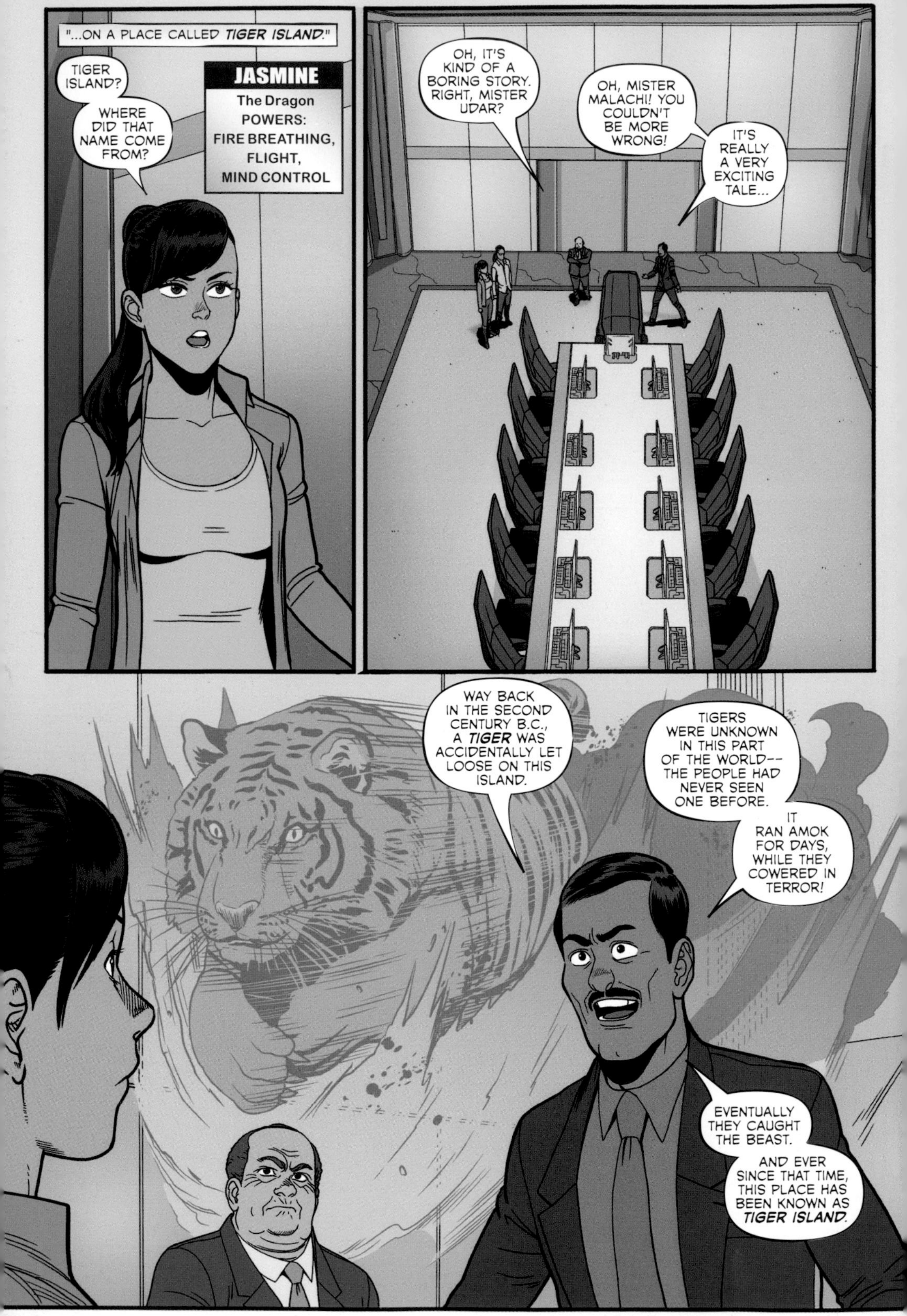
"...ON A PLACE CALLED TIGER ISLAND."
TIGER ISLAND?
WHERE DID THAT NAME COME FROM?
JASMINE
The Dragon
POWERS:
FIRE BREATHING,
FLIGHT,
MIND CONTROL
OH, IT'S KIND OF A BORING STORY. RIGHT, MISTER UDAR?
OH, MISTER MALACHI! YOU COULDN'T BE MORE WRONG!
IT'S REALLY A VERY EXCITING TALE...
WAY BACK IN THE SECOND CENTURY B.C., A TIGER WAS ACCIDENTALLY LET LOOSE ON THIS ISLAND.
TIGERS WERE UNKNOWN IN THIS PART OF THE WORLD-- THE PEOPLE HAD NEVER SEEN ONE BEFORE.
IT RAN AMOK FOR DAYS, WHILE THEY COWERED IN TERROR!
EVENTUALLY THEY CAUGHT THE BEAST.
AND EVER SINCE THAT TIME, THIS PLACE HAS BEEN KNOWN AS TIGER ISLAND.

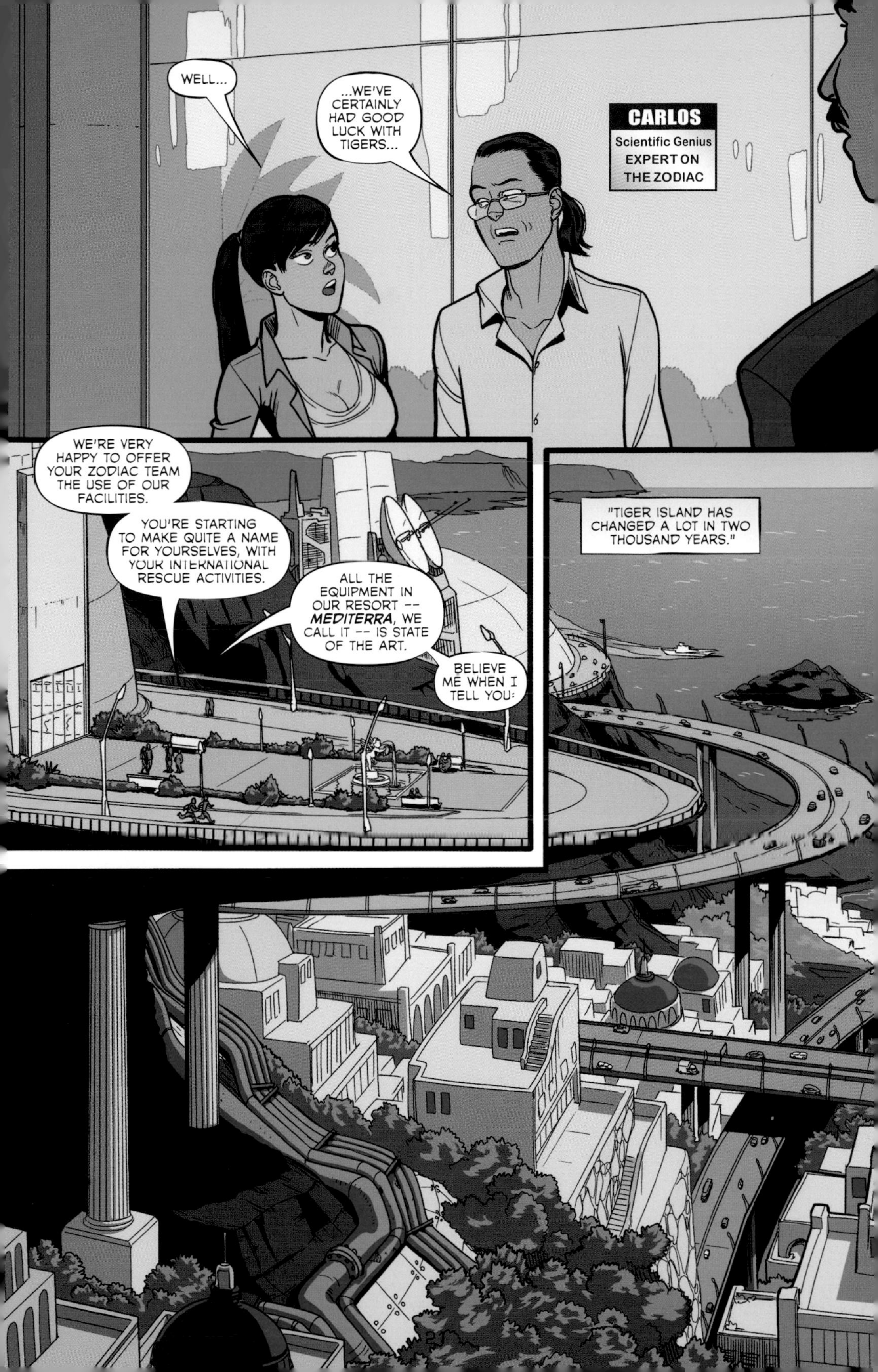
WELL...
...WE'VE CERTAINLY HAD GOOD LUCK WITH TIGERS...
CARLOS
Scientific Genius
EXPERT ON THE ZODIAC
WE'RE VERY HAPPY TO OFFER YOUR ZODIAC TEAM THE USE OF OUR FACILITIES.
YOU'RE STARTING TO MAKE QUITE A NAME FOR YOURSELVES, WITH YOUR INTERNATIONAL RESCUE ACTIVITIES.
ALL THE EQUIPMENT IN OUR RESORT -- *MEDITERRA*, WE CALL IT -- IS STATE OF THE ART.
BELIEVE ME WHEN I TELL YOU:
"TIGER ISLAND HAS CHANGED A LOT IN TWO THOUSAND YEARS."

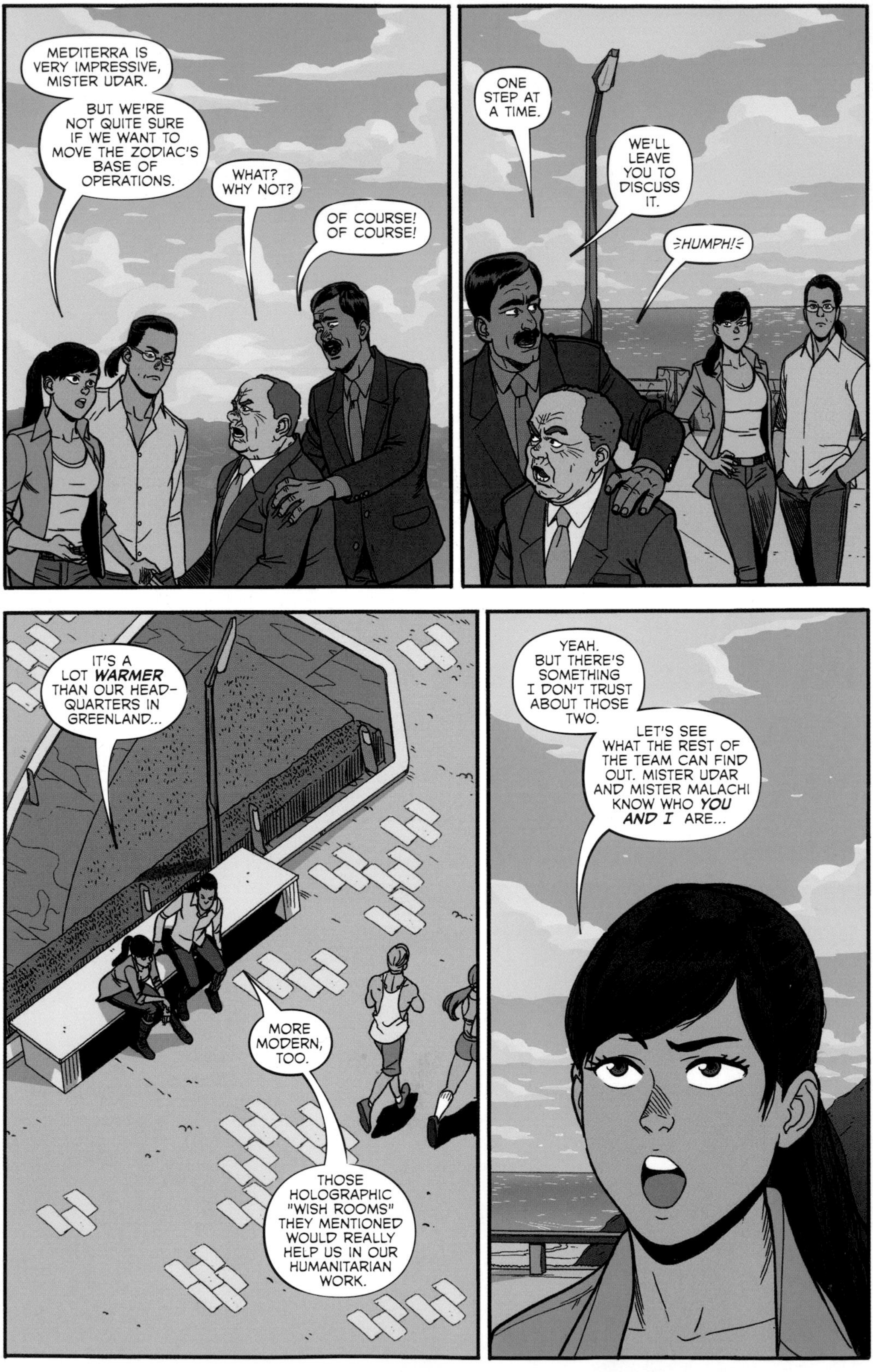
MEDITERRA IS VERY IMPRESSIVE, MISTER UDAR.
BUT WE'RE NOT QUITE SURE IF WE WANT TO MOVE THE ZODIAC'S BASE OF OPERATIONS.
WHAT? WHY NOT?
OF COURSE! OF COURSE!
ONE STEP AT A TIME.
WE'LL LEAVE YOU TO DISCUSS IT.
HUMPH!
IT'S A LOT WARMER THAN OUR HEAD-QUARTERS IN GREENLAND...
MORE MODERN, TOO.
THOSE HOLOGRAPHIC "WISH ROOMS" THEY MENTIONED WOULD REALLY HELP US IN OUR HUMANITARIAN WORK.
YEAH. BUT THERE'S SOMETHING I DON'T TRUST ABOUT THOSE TWO.
LET'S SEE WHAT THE REST OF THE TEAM CAN FIND OUT. MISTER UDAR AND MISTER MALACHI KNOW WHO YOU AND I ARE...

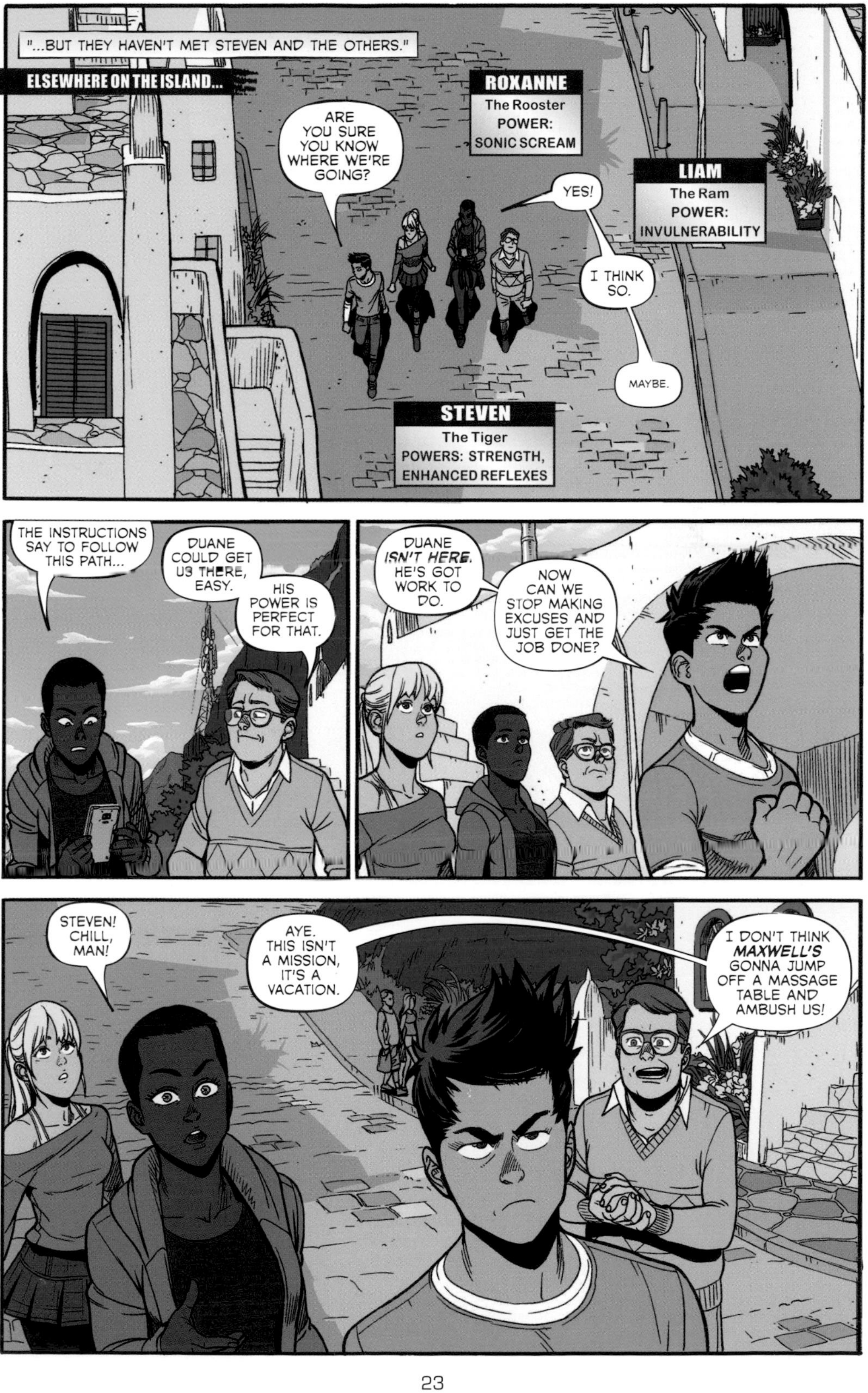
"...BUT THEY HAVEN'T MET STEVEN AND THE OTHERS."
ELSEWHERE ON THE ISLAND...
ROXANNE
The Rooster
POWER:
SONIC SCREAM
ARE YOU SURE YOU KNOW WHERE WE'RE GOING?
LIAM
The Ram
POWER:
INVULNERABILITY
YES!
I THINK SO.
MAYBE.
STEVEN
The Tiger
POWERS: STRENGTH,
ENHANCED REFLEXES
THE INSTRUCTIONS SAY TO FOLLOW THIS PATH...
DUANE COULD GET US THERE, EASY.
HIS POWER IS PERFECT FOR THAT.
DUANE *ISN'T HERE*. HE'S GOT WORK TO DO.
NOW CAN WE STOP MAKING EXCUSES AND JUST GET THE JOB DONE?
STEVEN! CHILL, MAN!
AYE. THIS ISN'T A MISSION, IT'S A VACATION.
I DON'T THINK *MAXWELL'S* GONNA JUMP OFF A MASSAGE TABLE AND AMBUSH US!

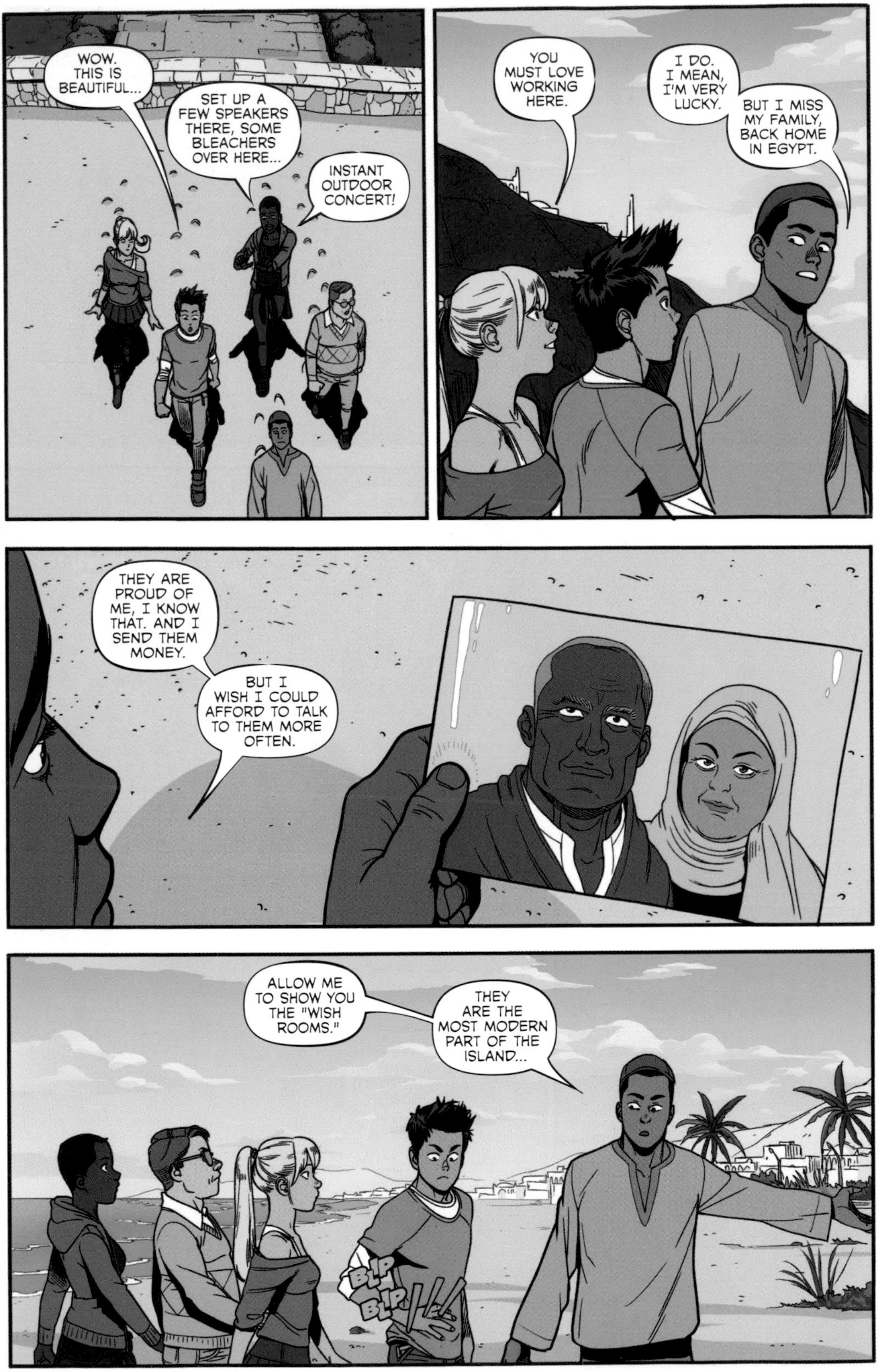
WOW. THIS IS BEAUTIFUL...
SET UP A FEW SPEAKERS THERE, SOME BLEACHERS OVER HERE...
INSTANT OUTDOOR CONCERT!
YOU MUST LOVE WORKING HERE.
I DO. I MEAN, I'M VERY LUCKY.
BUT I MISS MY FAMILY, BACK HOME IN EGYPT.
THEY ARE PROUD OF ME, I KNOW THAT. AND I SEND THEM MONEY.
BUT I WISH I COULD AFFORD TO TALK TO THEM MORE OFTEN.
ALLOW ME TO SHOW YOU THE "WISH ROOMS."
THEY ARE THE MOST MODERN PART OF THE ISLAND...
BLIP BLIP

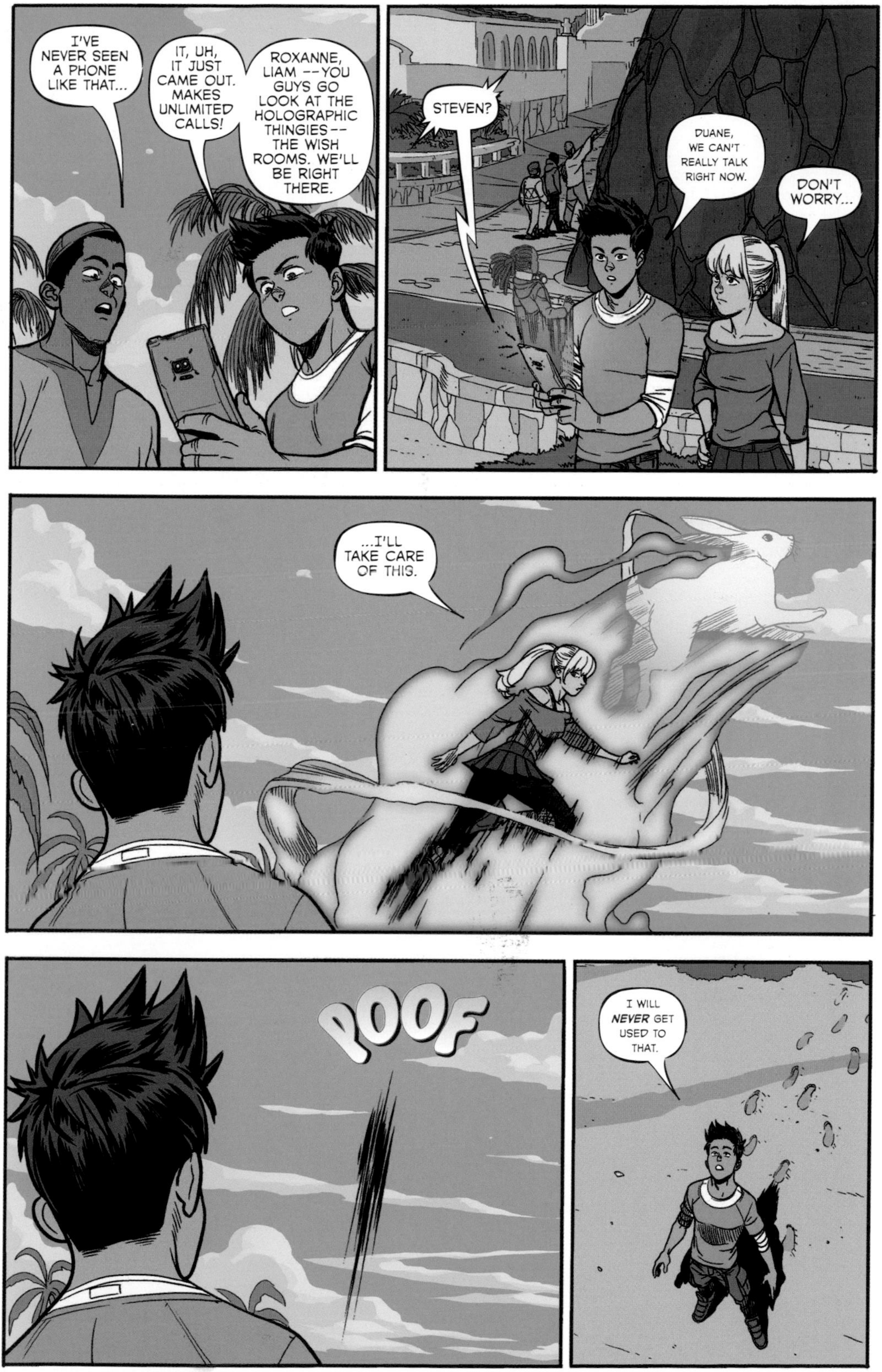
I'VE NEVER SEEN A PHONE LIKE THAT...
IT, UH, IT JUST CAME OUT. MAKES UNLIMITED CALLS!
ROXANNE, LIAM --YOU GUYS GO LOOK AT THE HOLOGRAPHIC THINGIES-- THE WISH ROOMS. WE'LL BE RIGHT THERE.
STEVEN?
DUANE, WE CAN'T REALLY TALK RIGHT NOW.
DON'T WORRY...
...I'LL TAKE CARE OF THIS.
POOF
I WILL NEVER GET USED TO THAT.

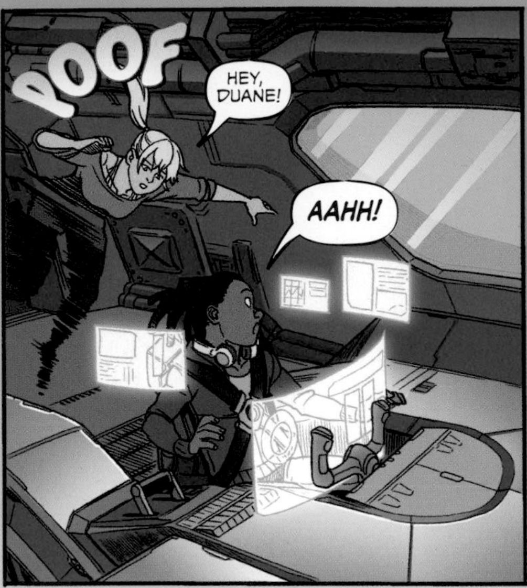
POOF
HEY, DUANE!
AAHH!

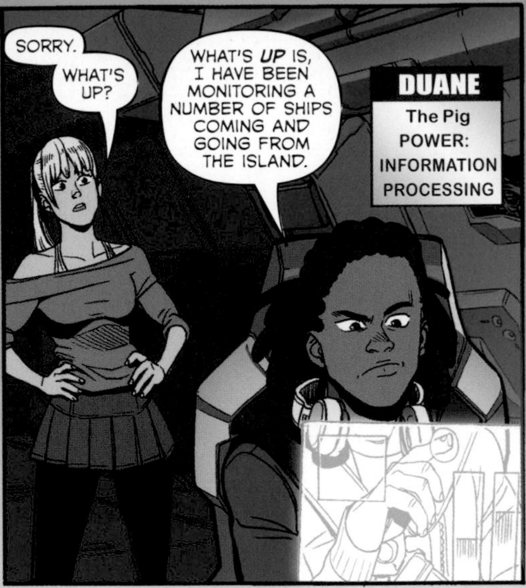
SORRY.
WHAT'S UP?
WHAT'S UP IS, I HAVE BEEN MONITORING A NUMBER OF SHIPS COMING AND GOING FROM THE ISLAND.
DUANE
The Pig
POWER: INFORMATION PROCESSING

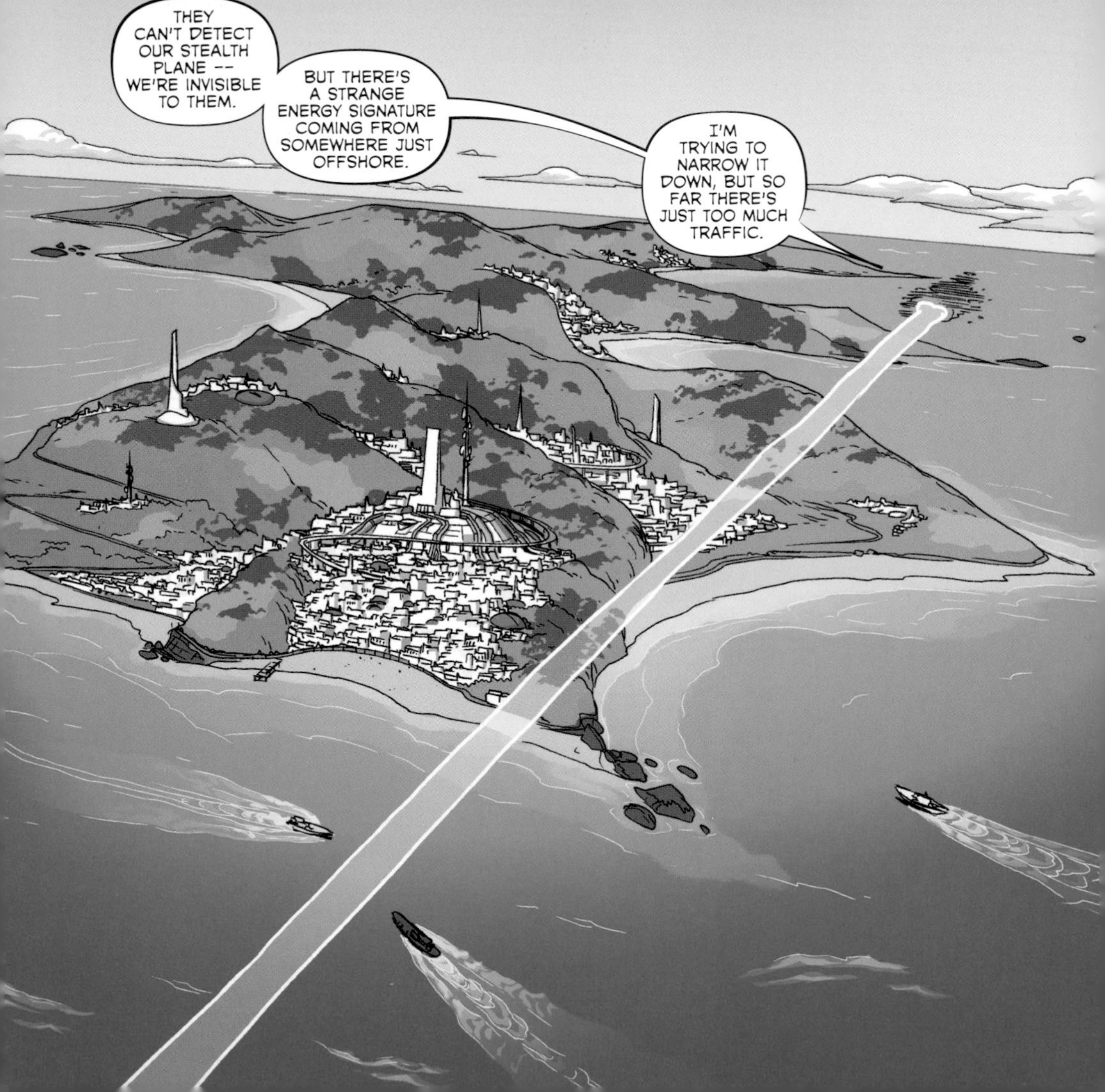
THEY CAN'T DETECT OUR STEALTH PLANE -- WE'RE INVISIBLE TO THEM.
BUT THERE'S A STRANGE ENERGY SIGNATURE COMING FROM SOMEWHERE JUST OFFSHORE.
I'M TRYING TO NARROW IT DOWN, BUT SO FAR THERE'S JUST TOO MUCH TRAFFIC.

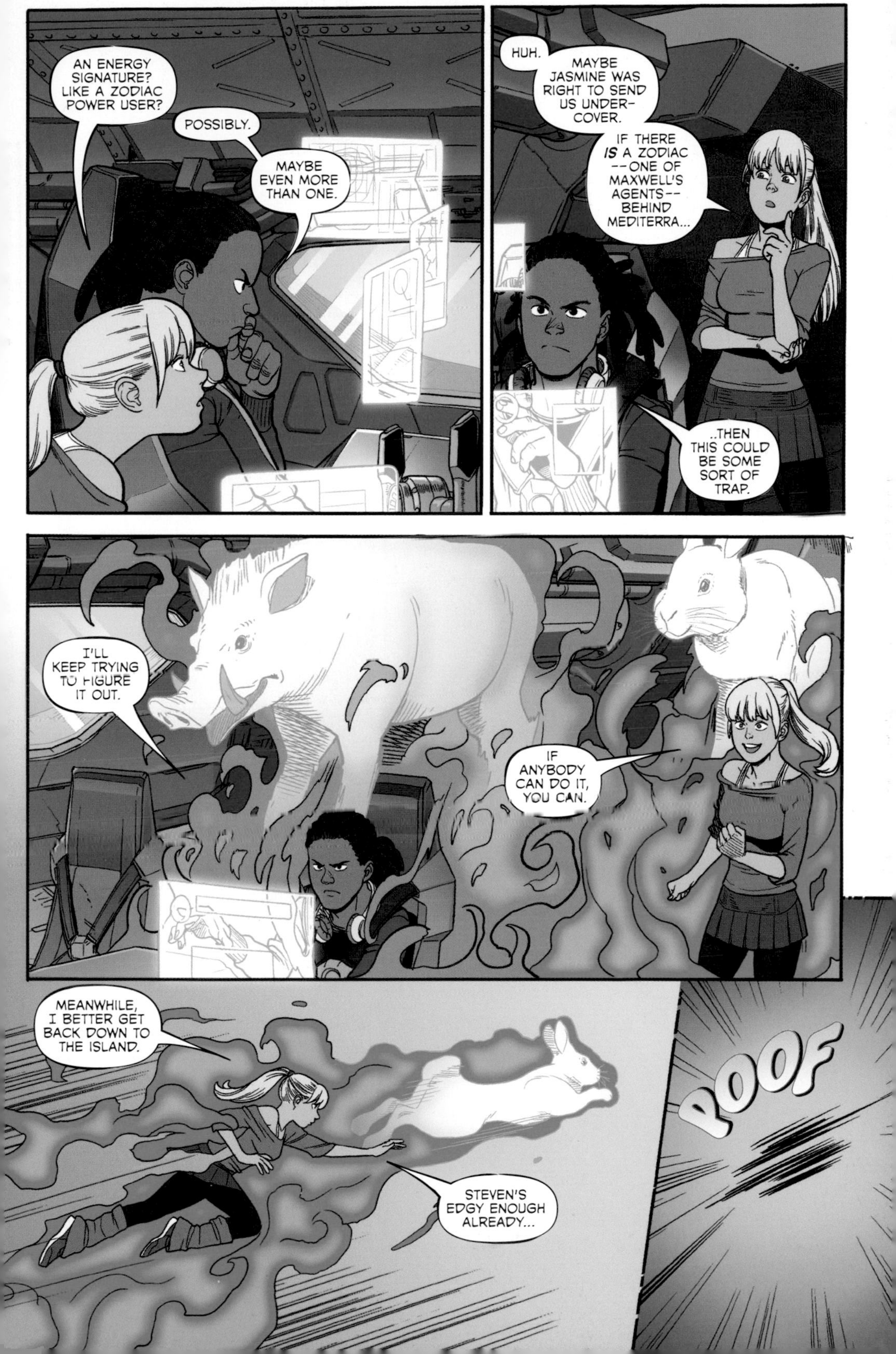
AN ENERGY SIGNATURE? LIKE A ZODIAC POWER USER?
POSSIBLY.
MAYBE EVEN MORE THAN ONE.
HUH.
MAYBE JASMINE WAS RIGHT TO SEND US UNDER-COVER.
IF THERE IS A ZODIAC --ONE OF MAXWELL'S AGENTS-- BEHIND MEDITERRA...
..THEN THIS COULD BE SOME SORT OF TRAP.
I'LL KEEP TRYING TO FIGURE IT OUT.
IF ANYBODY CAN DO IT, YOU CAN.
MEANWHILE, I BETTER GET BACK DOWN TO THE ISLAND.
STEVEN'S EDGY ENOUGH ALREADY...
POOF

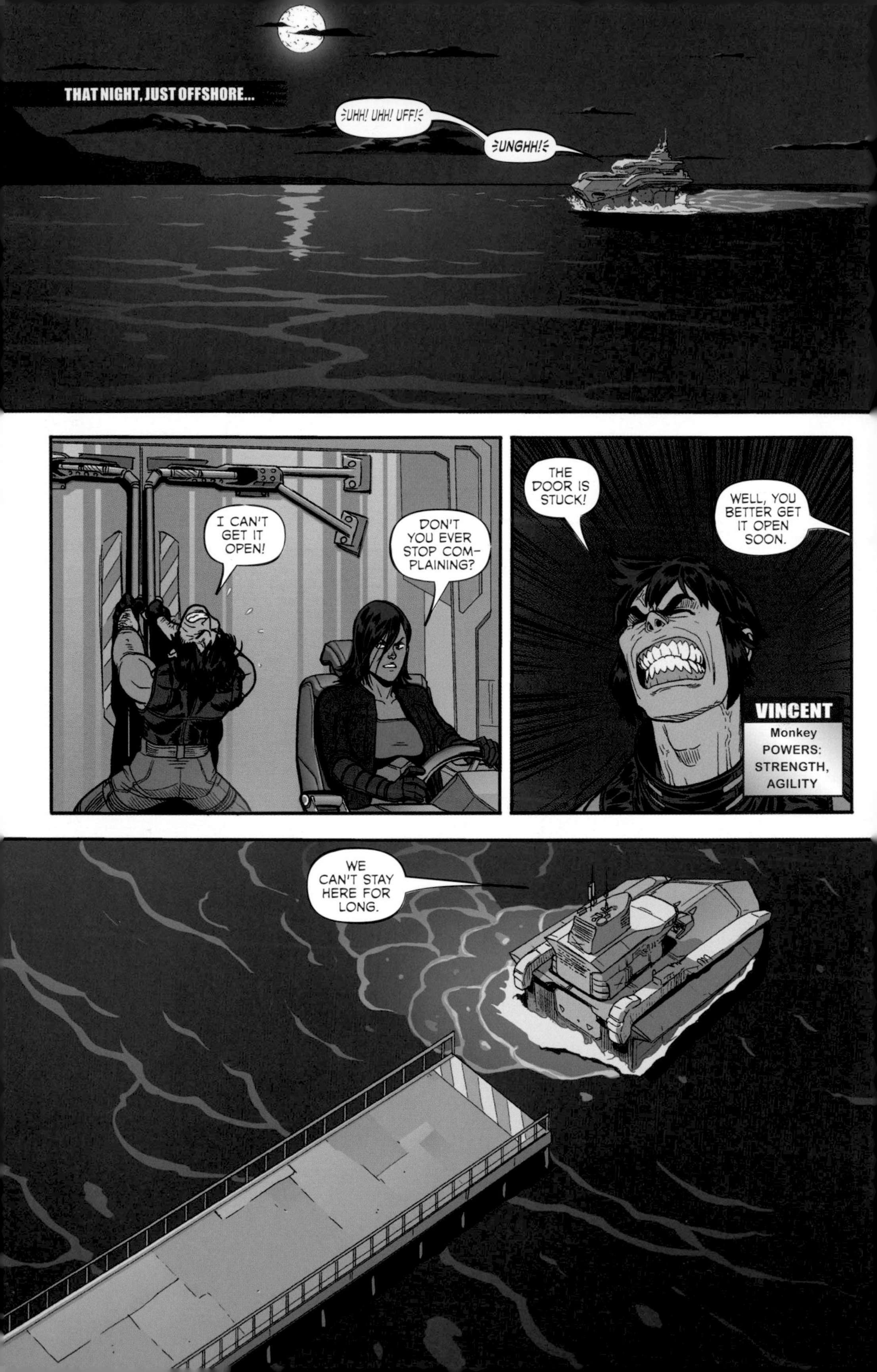
THAT NIGHT, JUST OFFSHORE...
UHH! UHH! UFF!
UNGHH!
I CAN'T GET IT OPEN!
DON'T YOU EVER STOP COM-PLAINING?
THE DOOR IS STUCK!
WELL, YOU BETTER GET IT OPEN SOON.
VINCENT
Monkey
POWERS: STRENGTH, AGILITY
WE CAN'T STAY HERE FOR LONG.

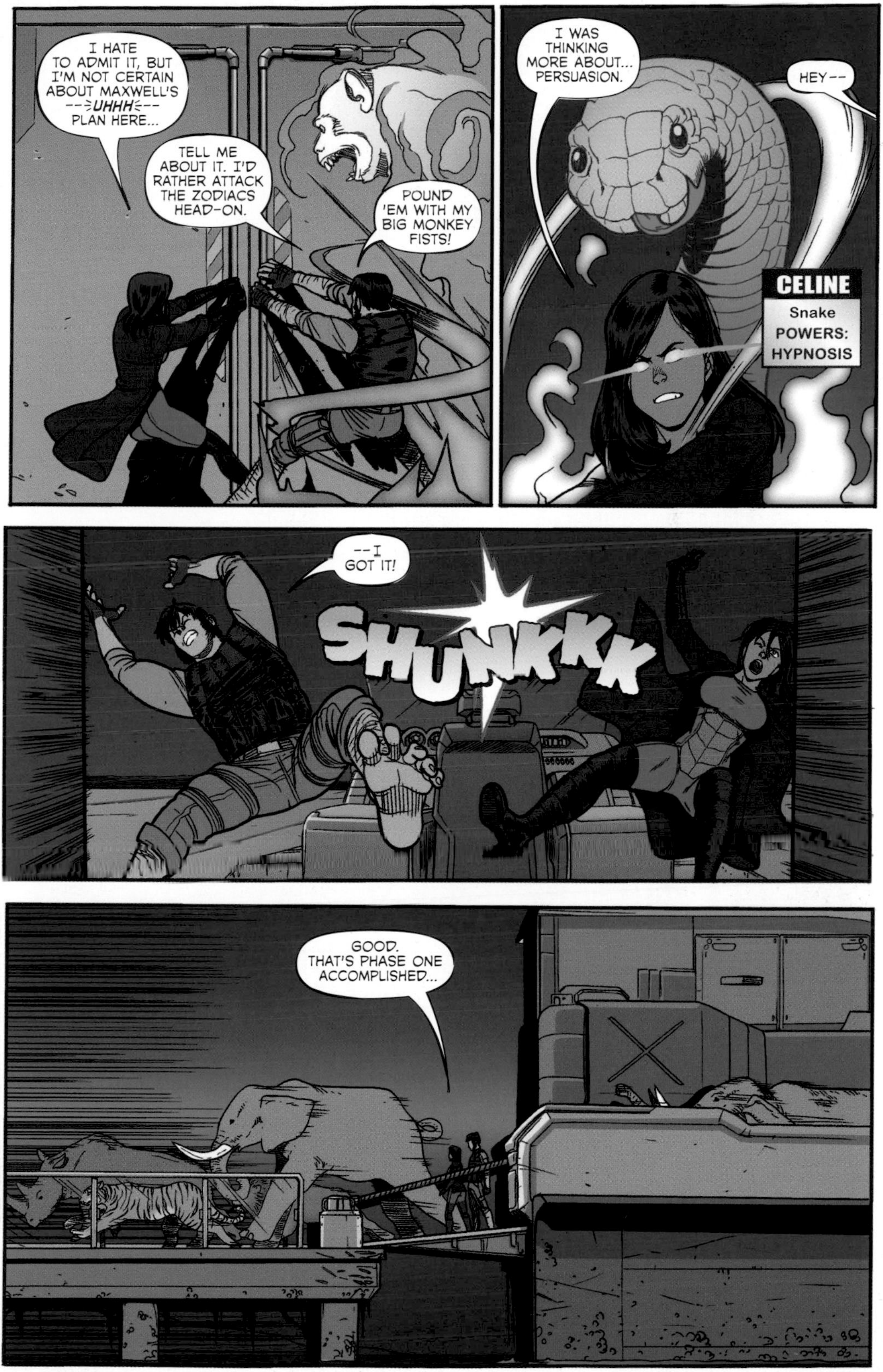
I HATE TO ADMIT IT, BUT I'M NOT CERTAIN ABOUT MAXWELL'S --UHHH-- PLAN HERE...
TELL ME ABOUT IT. I'D RATHER ATTACK THE ZODIACS HEAD-ON.
POUND 'EM WITH MY BIG MONKEY FISTS!
I WAS THINKING MORE ABOUT... PERSUASION.
HEY--
CELINE
Snake
POWERS: HYPNOSIS
--I GOT IT!
SHUNKKK
GOOD. THAT'S PHASE ONE ACCOMPLISHED...

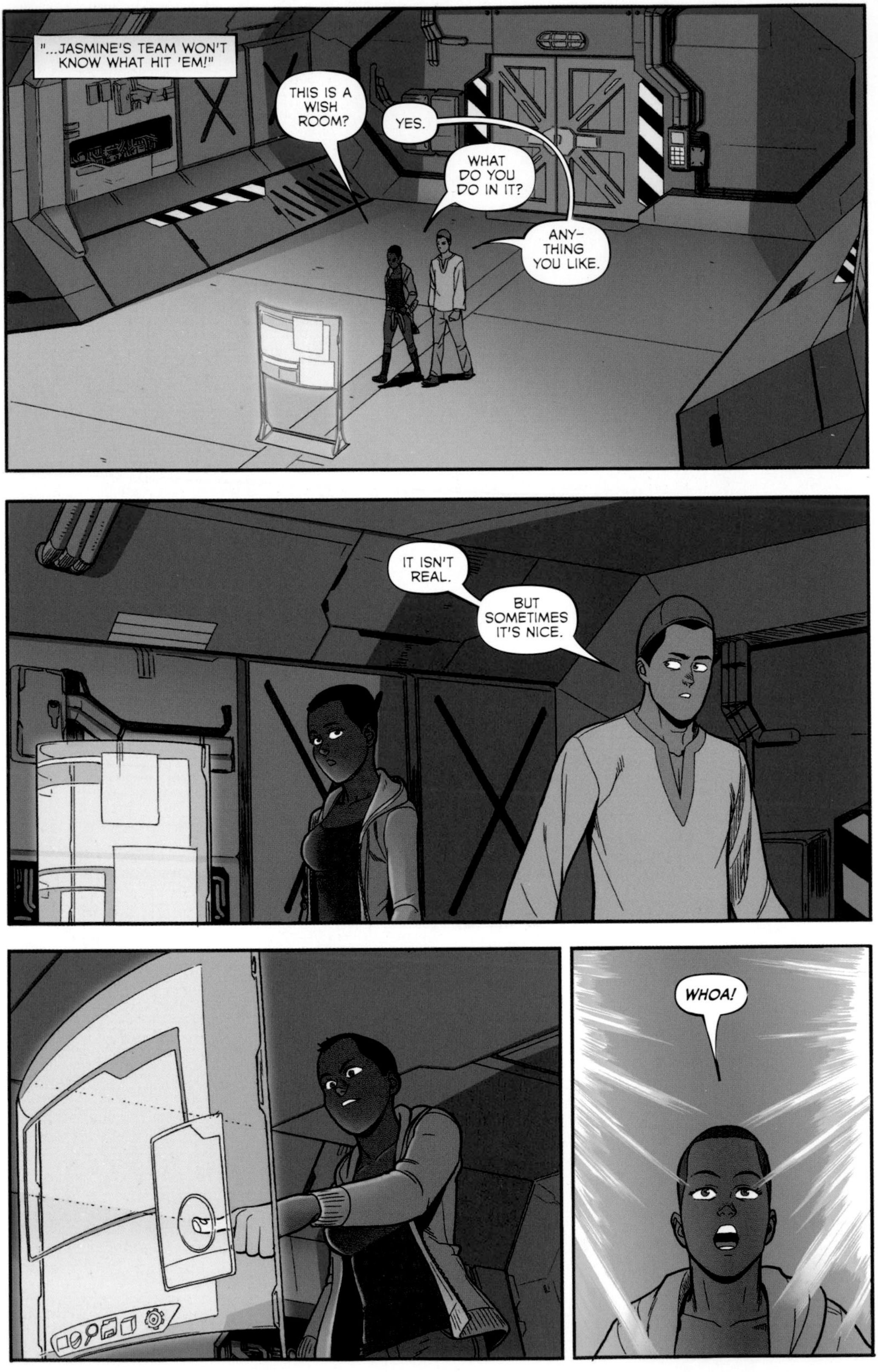
"...JASMINE'S TEAM WON'T KNOW WHAT HIT 'EM!"
THIS IS A WISH ROOM?
YES.
WHAT DO YOU DO IN IT?
ANY-THING YOU LIKE.
IT ISN'T REAL.
BUT SOMETIMES IT'S NICE.
WHOA!

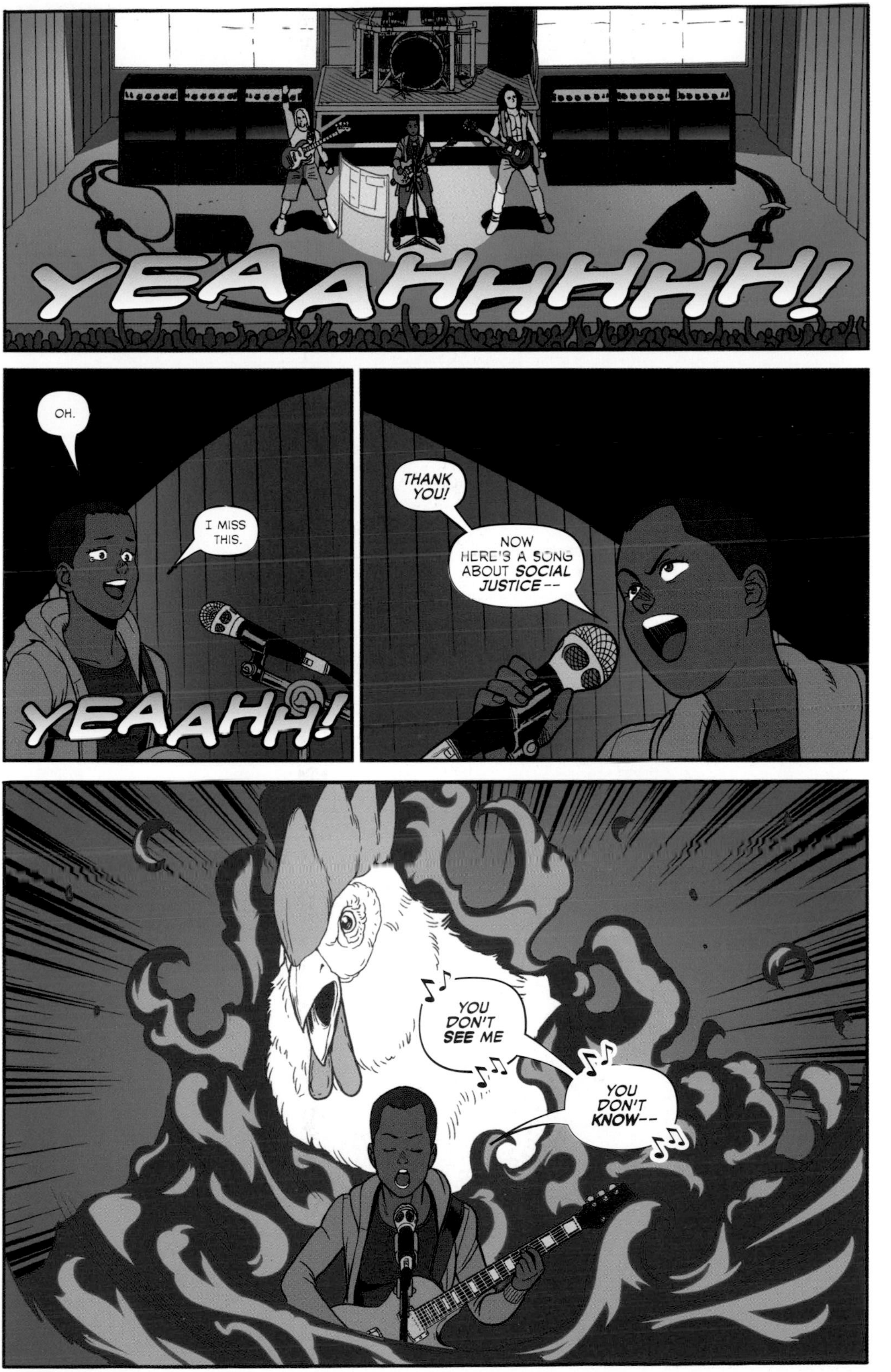
YEAAHHHHH!
OH.
I MISS THIS.
YEAAHH!
THANK YOU!
NOW HERE'S A SONG ABOUT SOCIAL JUSTICE--
YOU DON'T SEE ME
YOU DON'T KNOW--

HELP!

WHAT--

NO!

NO! IT'S JUST LIKE BEFORE-- WHEN I FIRST GOT MY ZODIAC POWER.

I CAN'T CONTROL IT...

GOT TO CHANGE IT.

CHANGE THE PROGRAM...

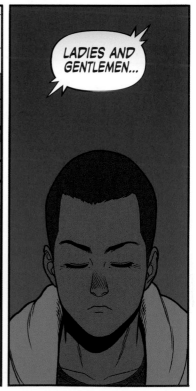

LADIES AND GENTLEMEN...

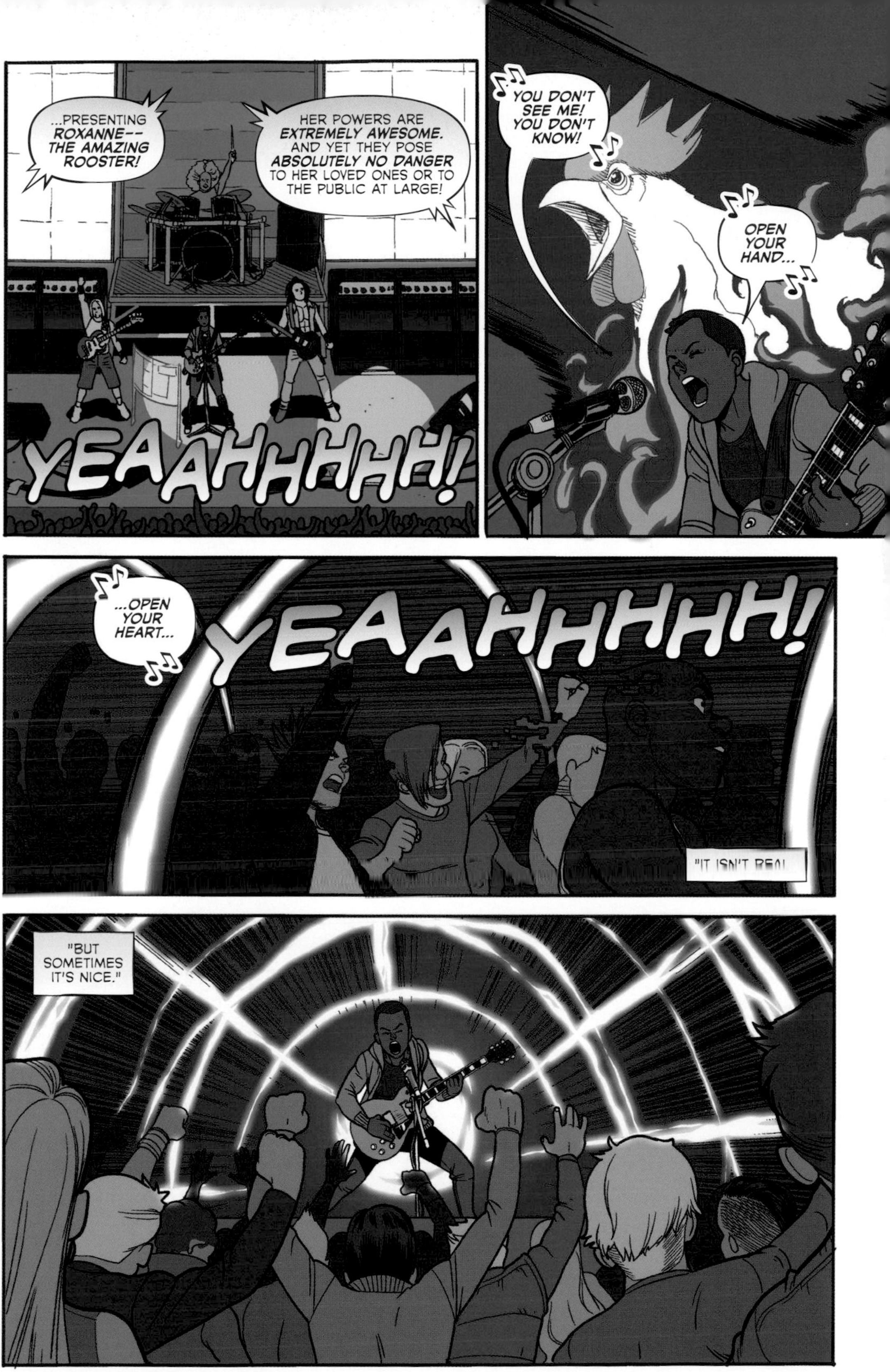
...PRESENTING ROXANNE-- THE AMAZING ROOSTER!
HER POWERS ARE EXTREMELY AWESOME. AND YET THEY POSE ABSOLUTELY NO DANGER TO HER LOVED ONES OR TO THE PUBLIC AT LARGE!
YEAAHHHHH!
YOU DON'T SEE ME! YOU DON'T KNOW!
OPEN YOUR HAND...
...OPEN YOUR HEART...
YEAAHHHHH!
"IT ISN'T REAL
"BUT SOMETIMES IT'S NICE."

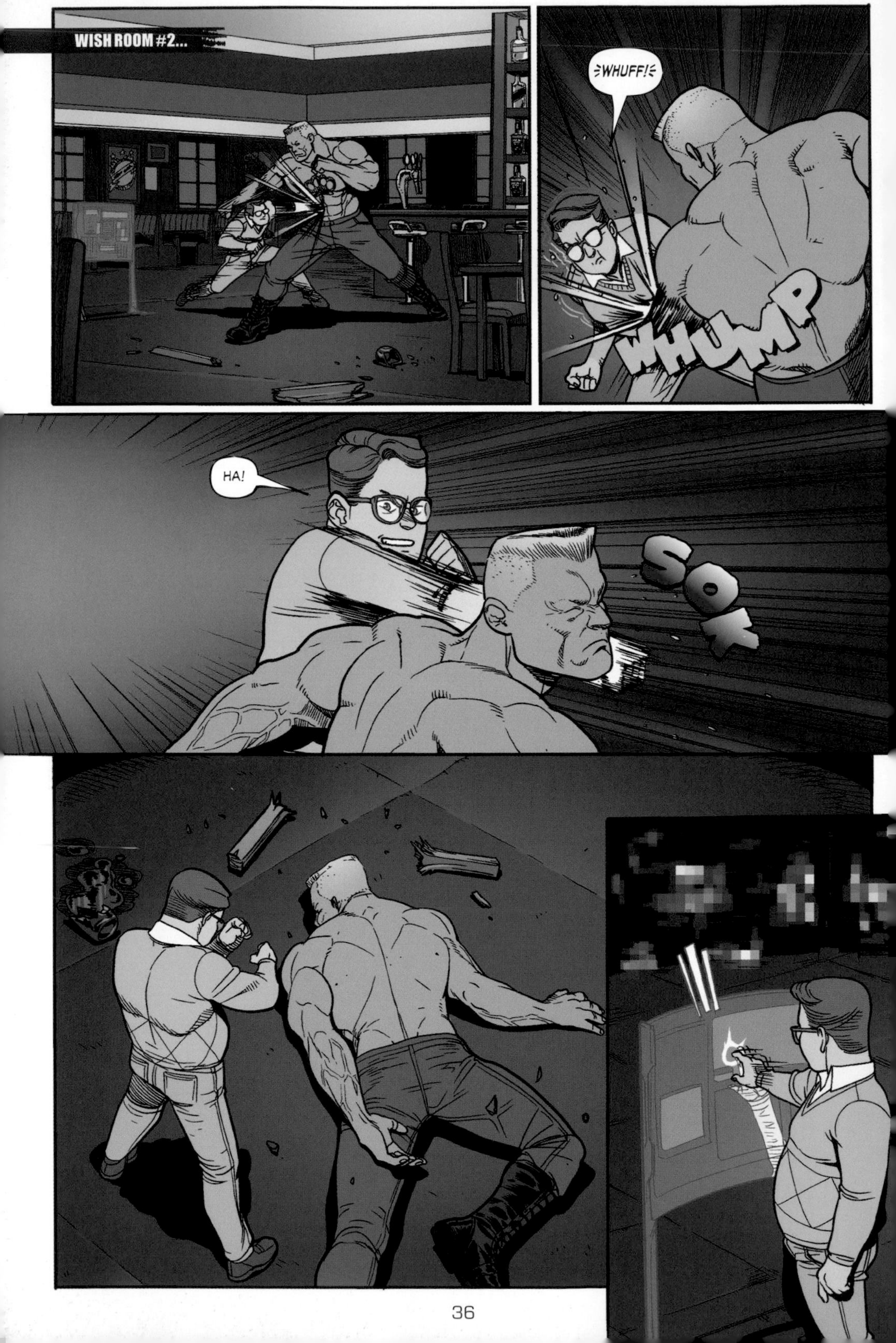
WISH ROOM #2...
WHUFF!
WHUMP
HA!
SOK

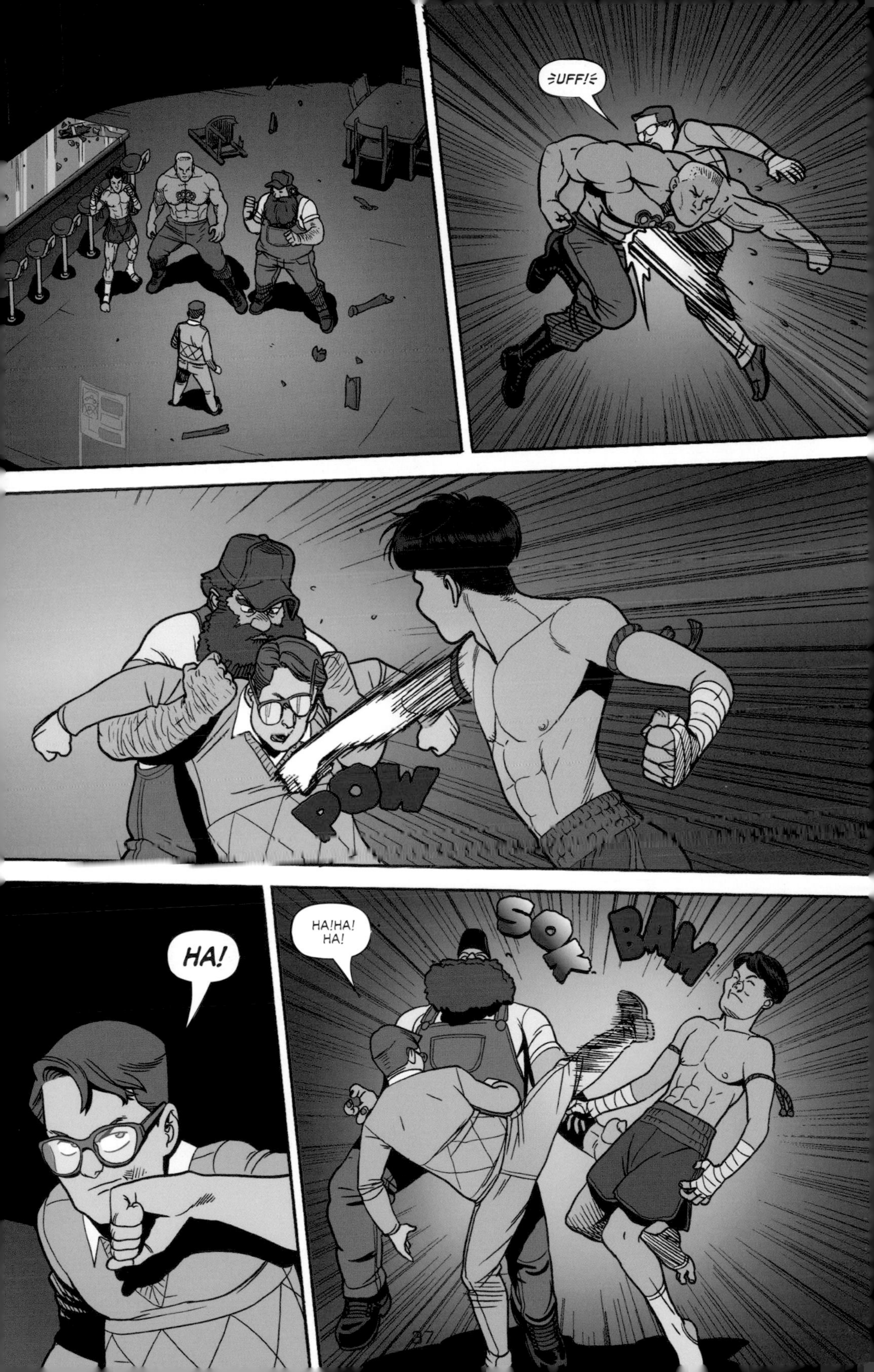
UFF!
POW
HA!
HA!HA! HA!
SOK
BAM

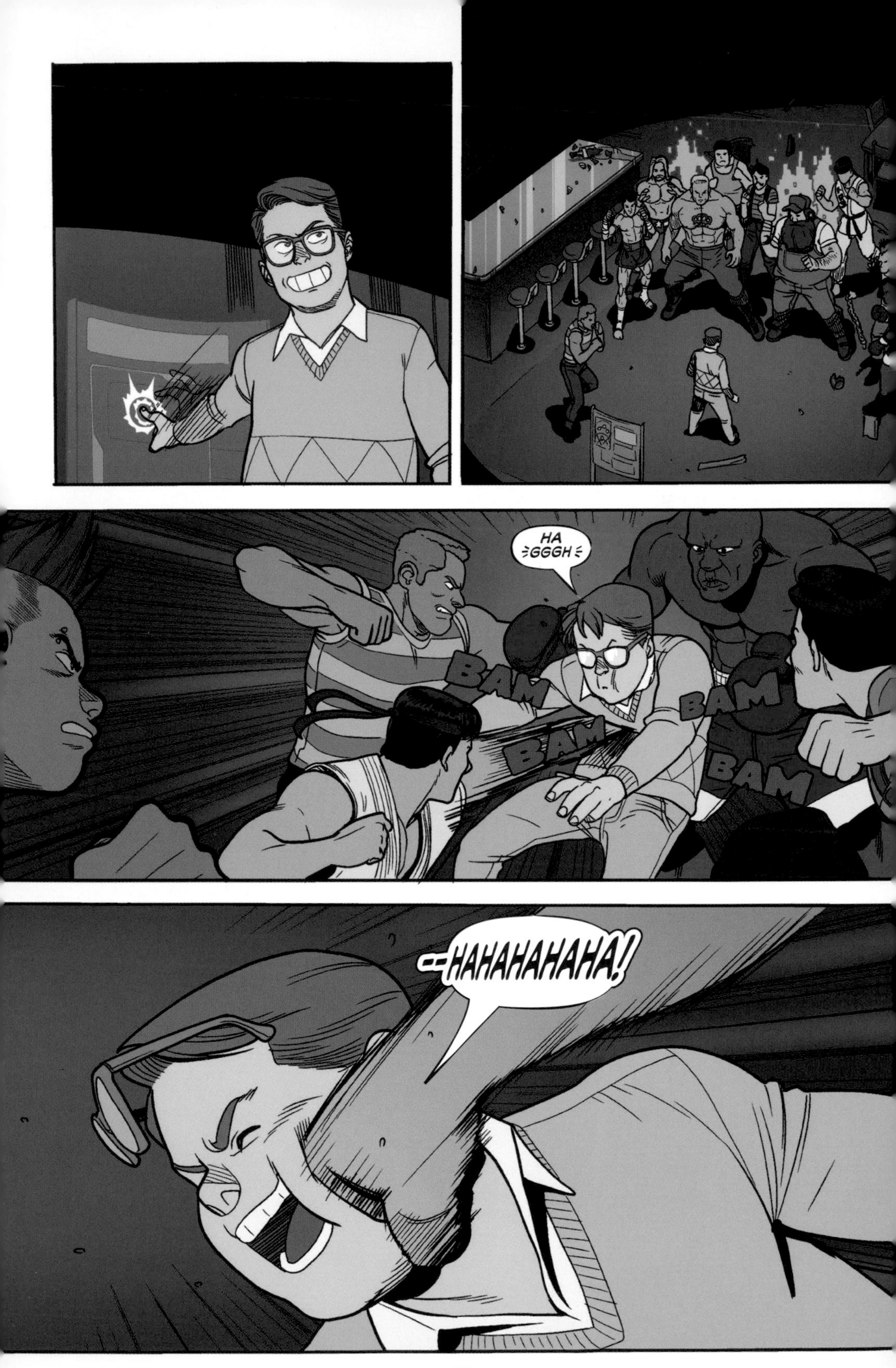
HA GGGH
BAM
BAM
BAM
BAM
--HAHAHAHAHA!

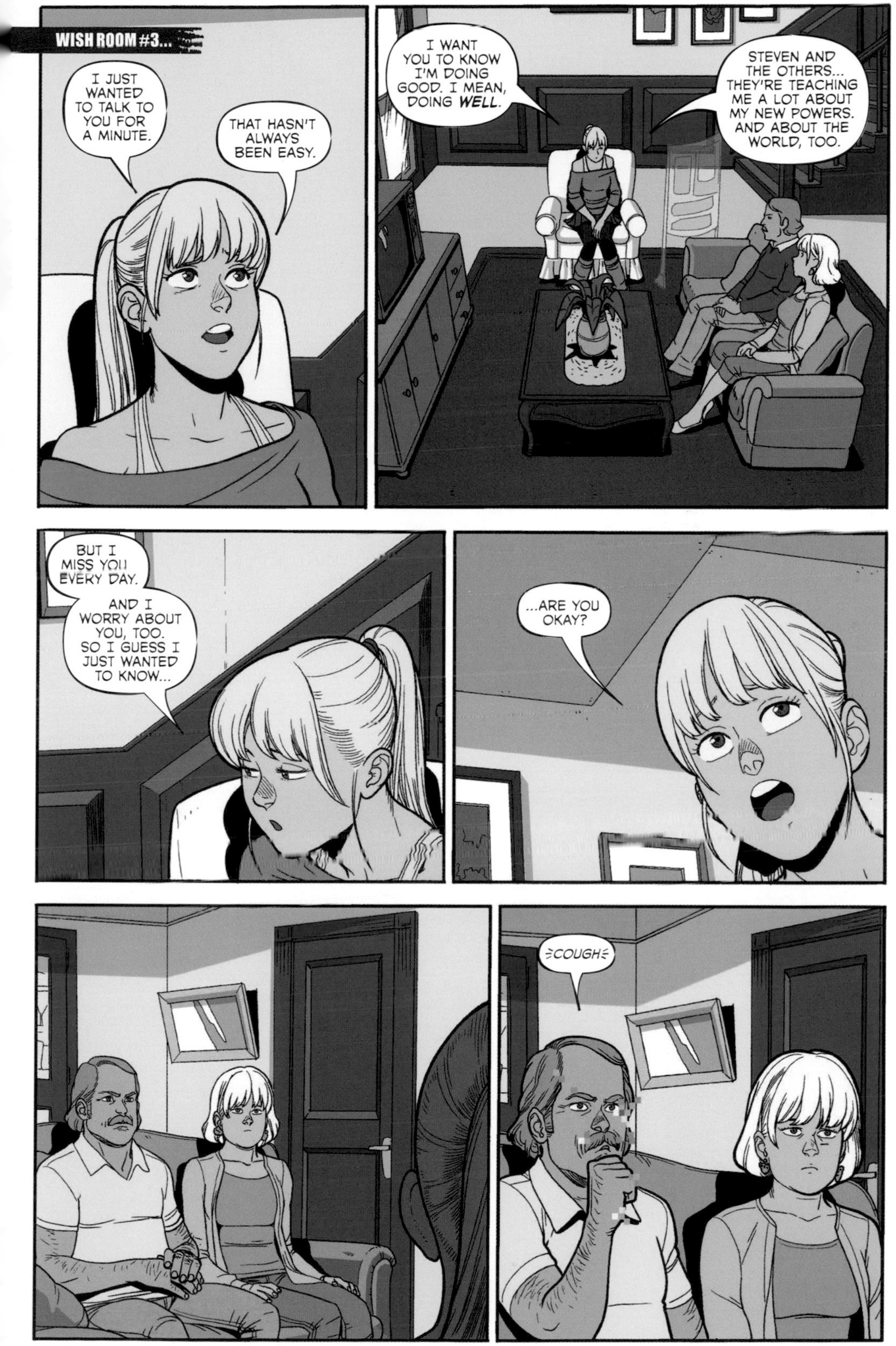
WISH ROOM #3...
I JUST WANTED TO TALK TO YOU FOR A MINUTE.
THAT HASN'T ALWAYS BEEN EASY.
I WANT YOU TO KNOW I'M DOING GOOD. I MEAN, DOING WELL.
STEVEN AND THE OTHERS... THEY'RE TEACHING ME A LOT ABOUT MY NEW POWERS. AND ABOUT THE WORLD, TOO.
BUT I MISS YOU EVERY DAY.
AND I WORRY ABOUT YOU, TOO. SO I GUESS I JUST WANTED TO KNOW...
...ARE YOU OKAY?
COUGH

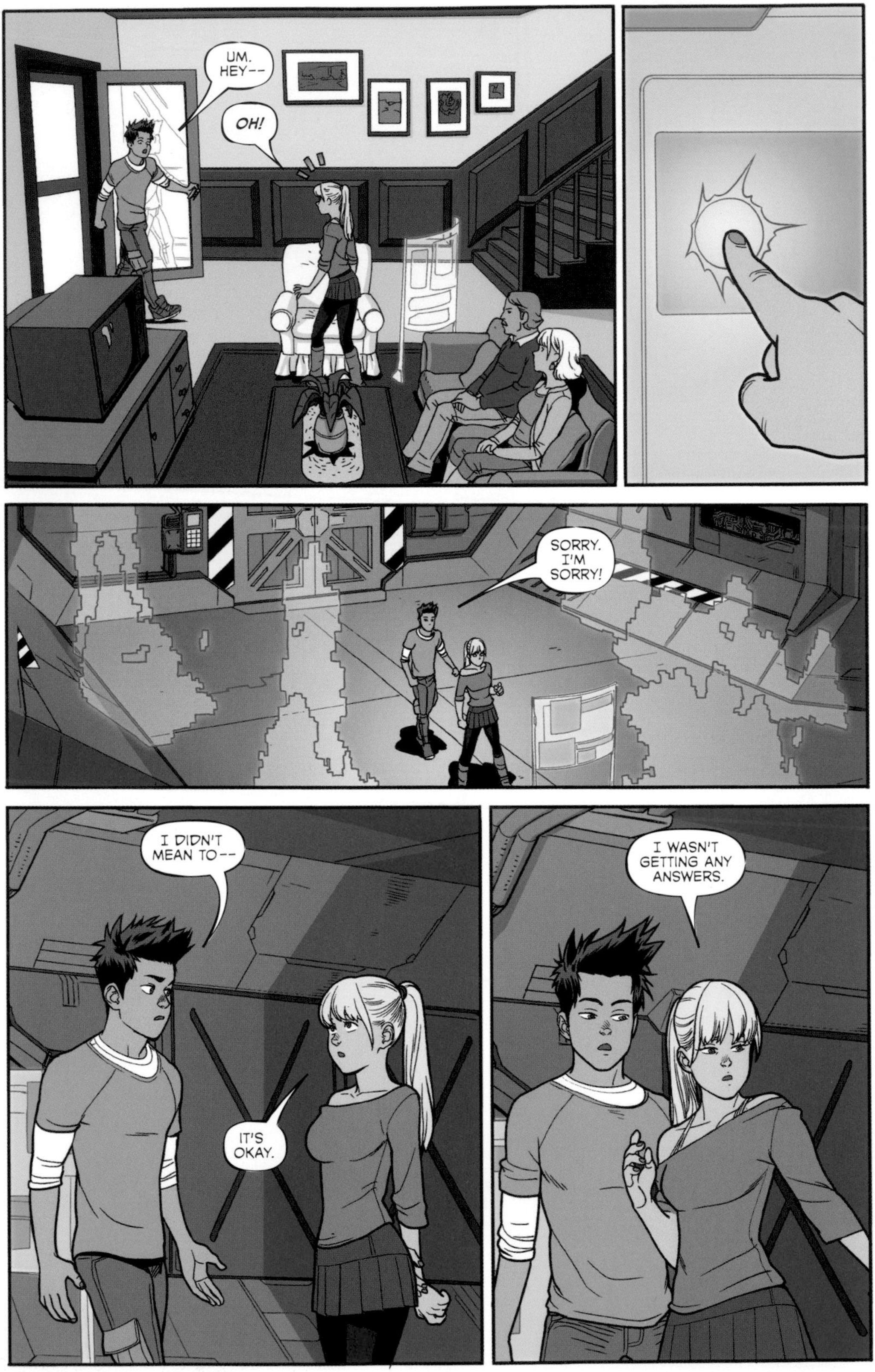
UM. HEY--
OH!
SORRY. I'M SORRY!
I DIDN'T MEAN TO--
IT'S OKAY.
I WASN'T GETTING ANY ANSWERS.

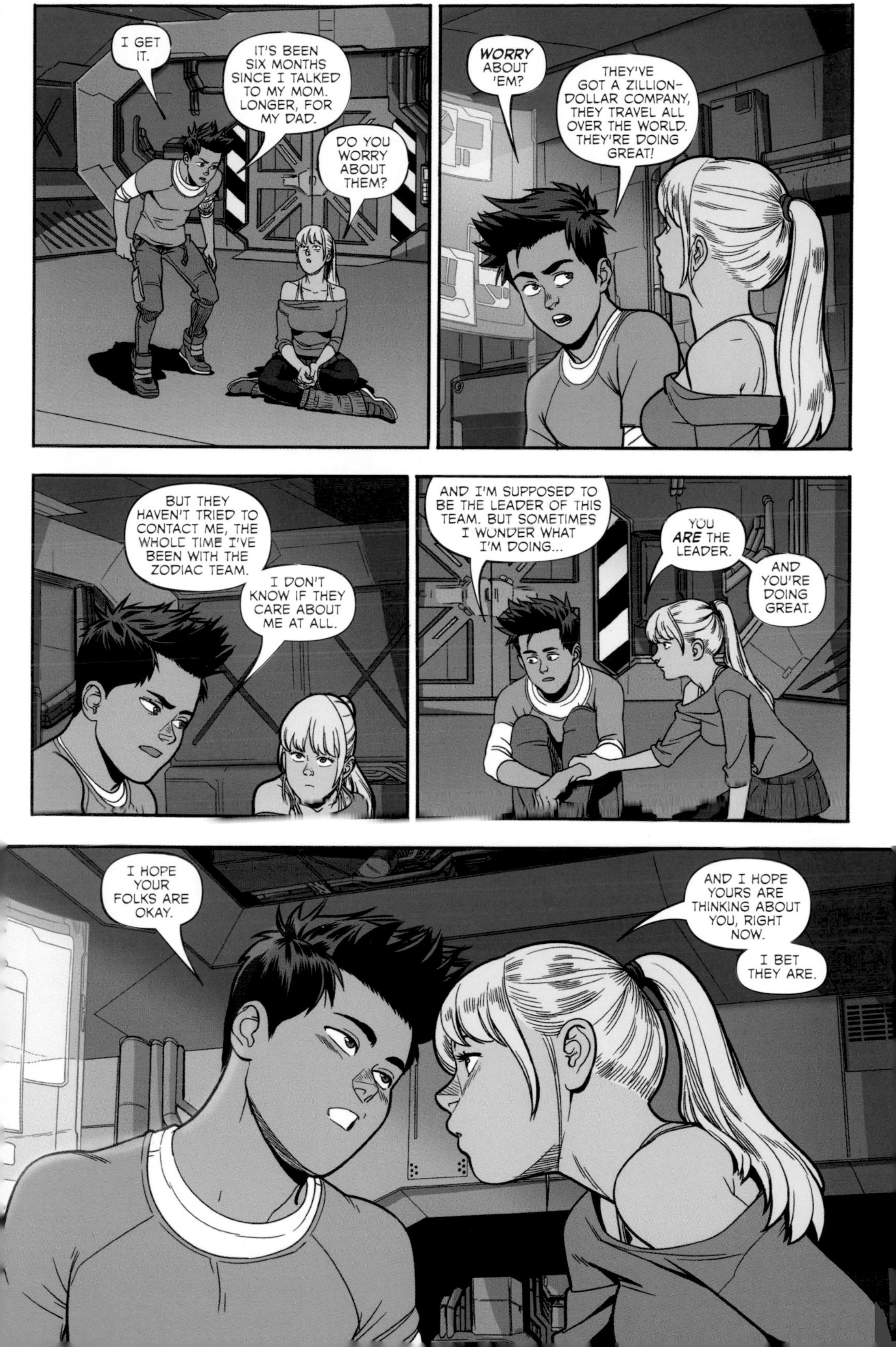
I GET IT.
IT'S BEEN SIX MONTHS SINCE I TALKED TO MY MOM. LONGER, FOR MY DAD.
DO YOU WORRY ABOUT THEM?
WORRY ABOUT 'EM?
THEY'VE GOT A ZILLION-DOLLAR COMPANY, THEY TRAVEL ALL OVER THE WORLD. THEY'RE DOING GREAT!
BUT THEY HAVEN'T TRIED TO CONTACT ME, THE WHOLE TIME I'VE BEEN WITH THE ZODIAC TEAM.
I DON'T KNOW IF THEY CARE ABOUT ME AT ALL.
AND I'M SUPPOSED TO BE THE LEADER OF THIS TEAM. BUT SOMETIMES I WONDER WHAT I'M DOING...
YOU ARE THE LEADER.
AND YOU'RE DOING GREAT.
I HOPE YOUR FOLKS ARE OKAY.
AND I HOPE YOURS ARE THINKING ABOUT YOU, RIGHT NOW.
I BET THEY ARE.

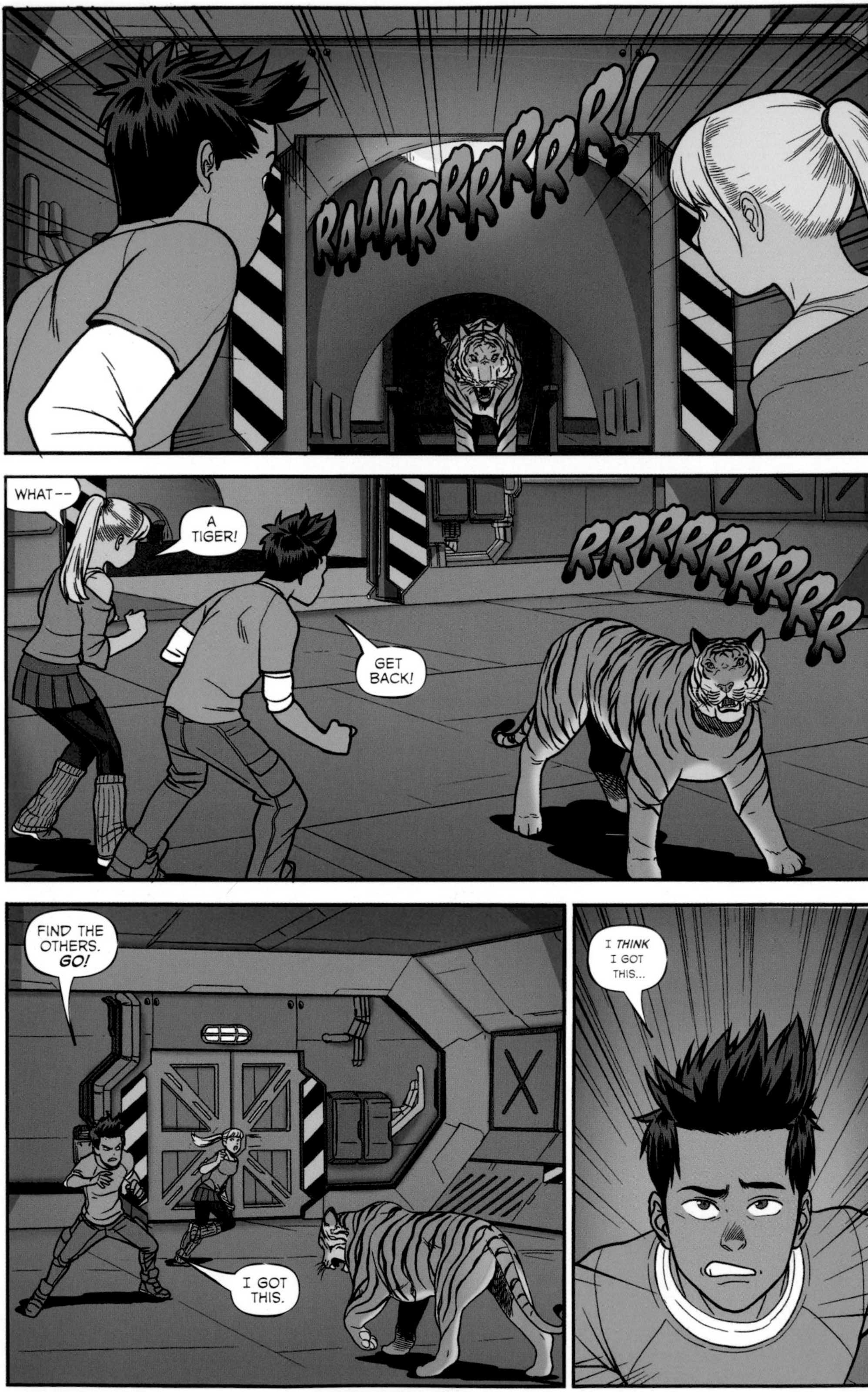
RAAARRRRRRR!
WHAT--
A TIGER!
RRRRRRRRRRR
GET BACK!
FIND THE OTHERS. *GO!*
I GOT THIS.
I *THINK* I GOT THIS...

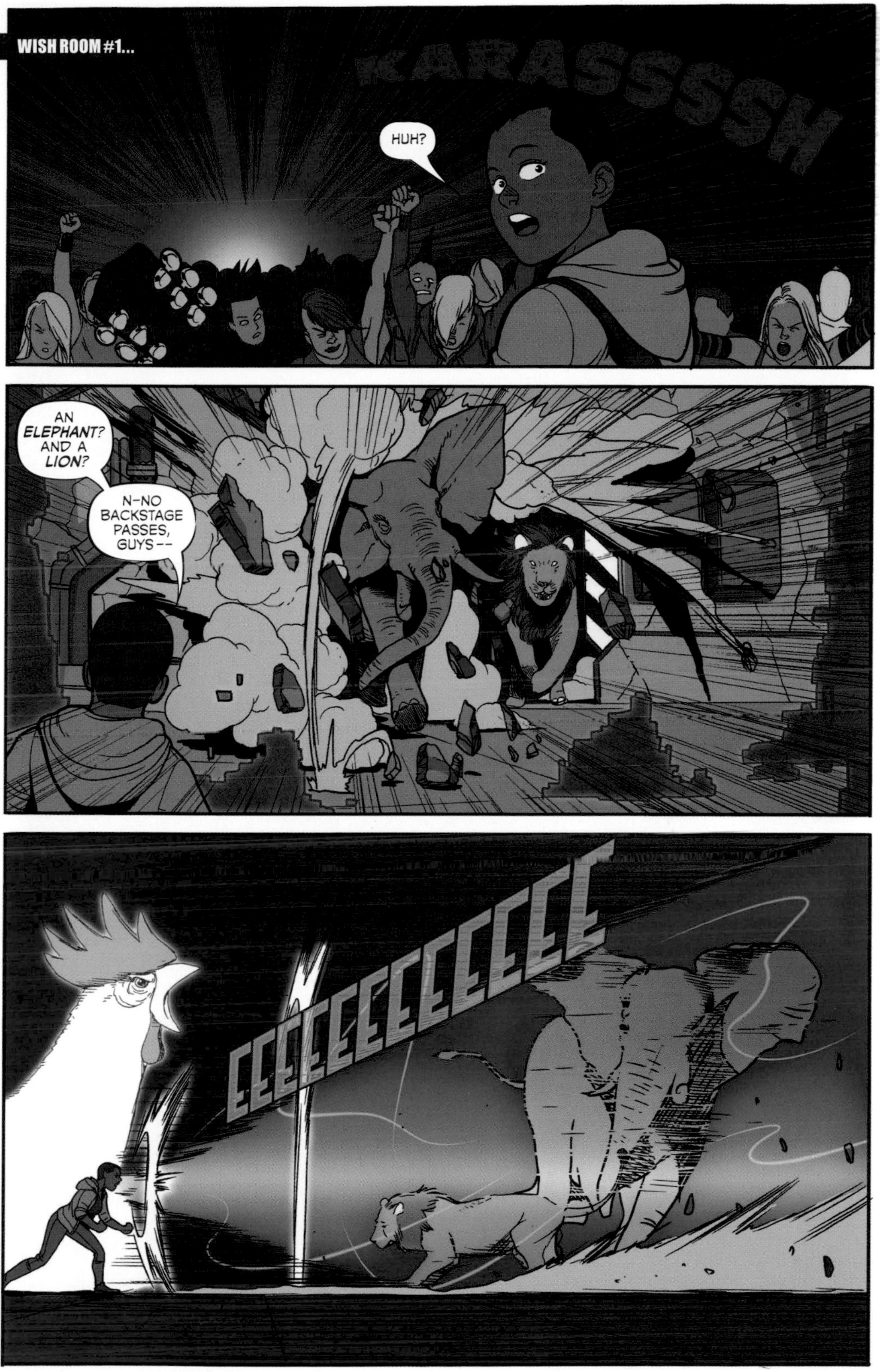
WISH ROOM #1...
KARASSSSSH
HUH?
AN ELEPHANT? AND A LION?
N-NO BACKSTAGE PASSES, GUYS--
EEEEEEEEEEEEE

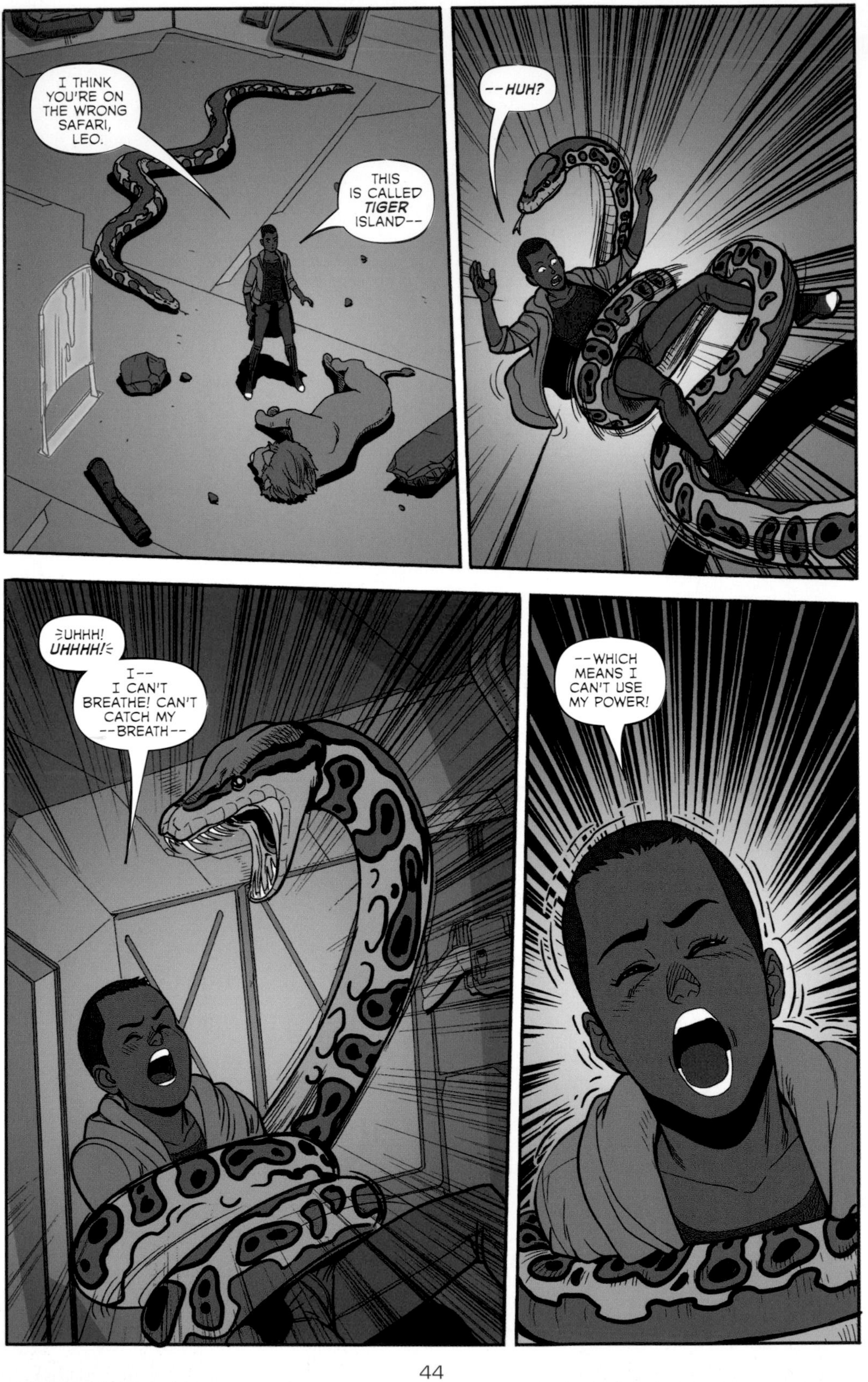
I THINK YOU'RE ON THE WRONG SAFARI, LEO.
THIS IS CALLED *TIGER* ISLAND--
--*HUH?*
UHHH! *UHHHH!*
I-- I CAN'T BREATHE! CAN'T CATCH MY --BREATH--
--WHICH MEANS I CAN'T USE MY POWER!

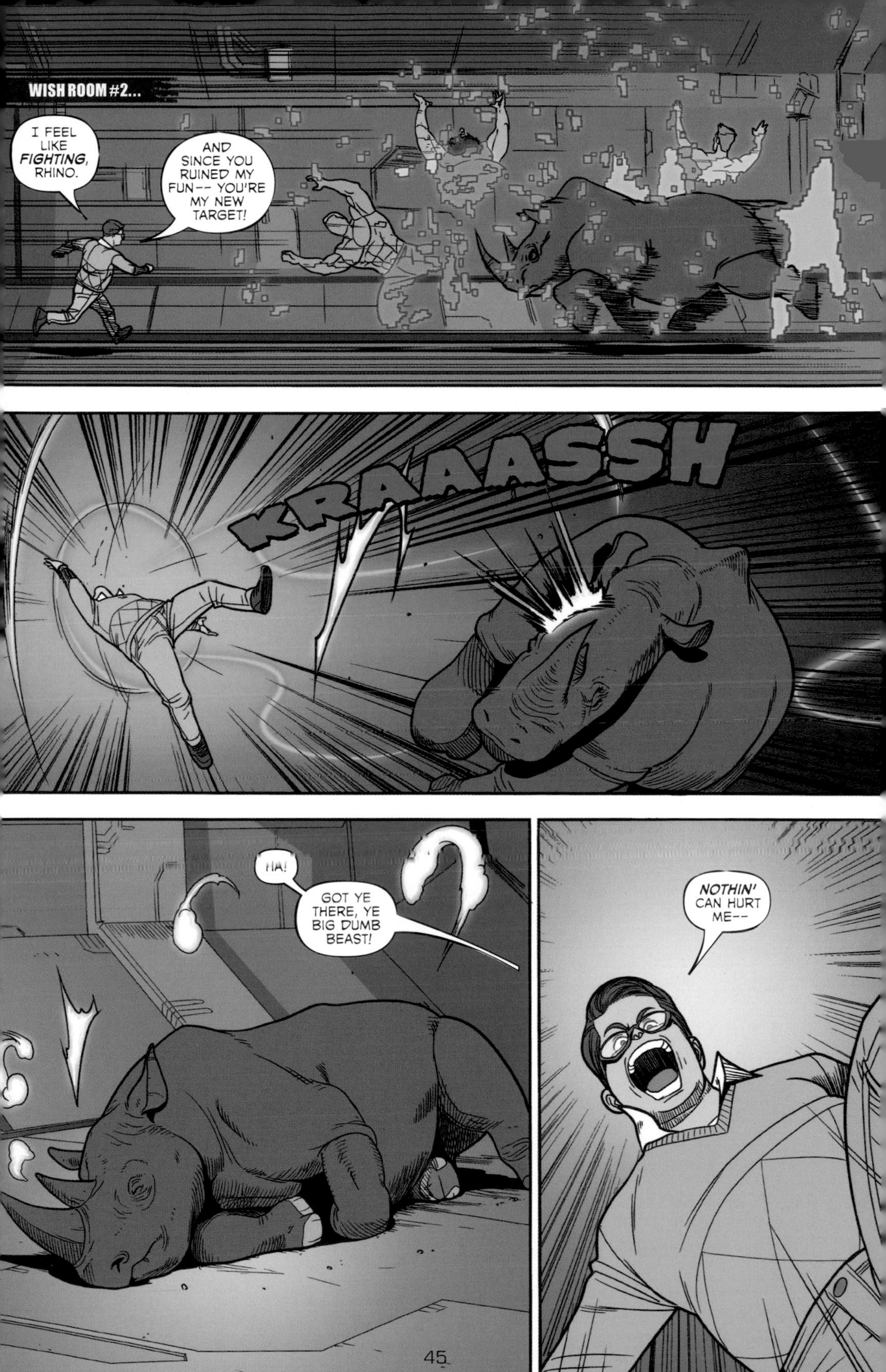
WISH ROOM #2...
I FEEL LIKE FIGHTING, RHINO.
AND SINCE YOU RUINED MY FUN-- YOU'RE MY NEW TARGET!
KRAAASSH
HA!
GOT YE THERE, YE BIG DUMB BEAST!
NOTHIN' CAN HURT ME--

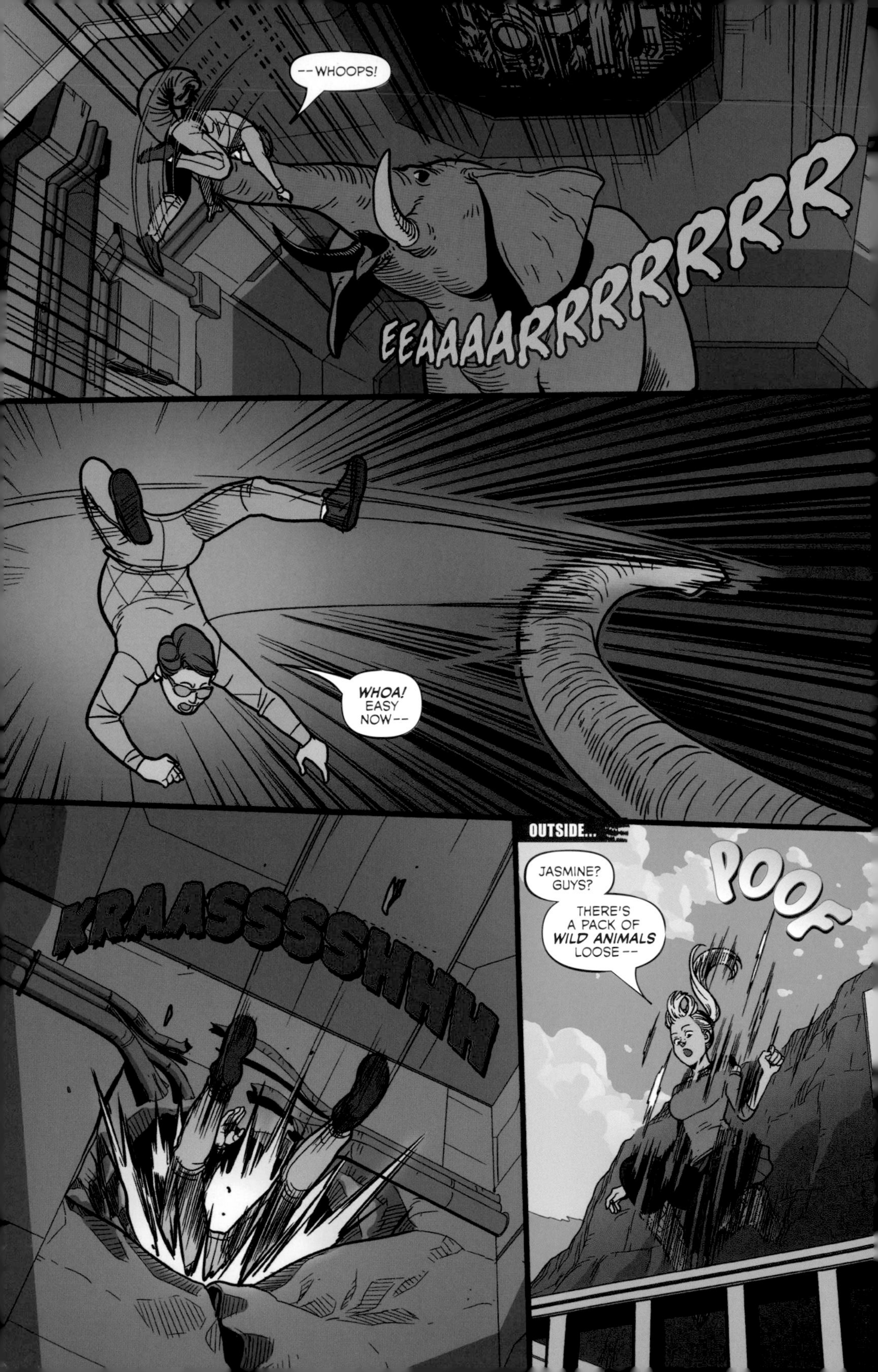

--WHOOPS!
EEAAAARRRRRRRR
WHOA! EASY NOW--
KRAASSSSSHHHH
OUTSIDE...
JASMINE? GUYS?
THERE'S A PACK OF WILD ANIMALS LOOSE --
POOF

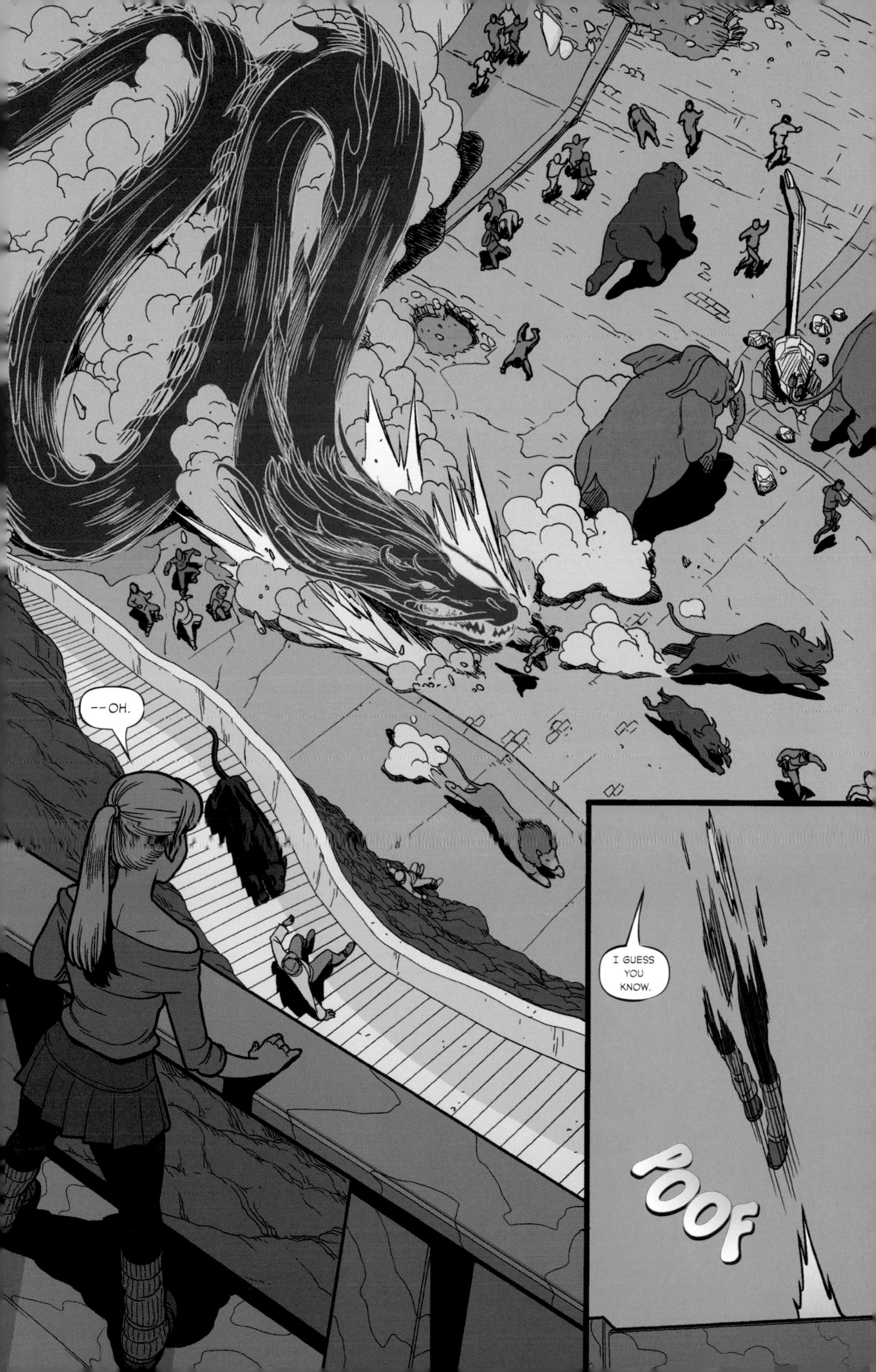
--OH.
I GUESS YOU KNOW.
POOF

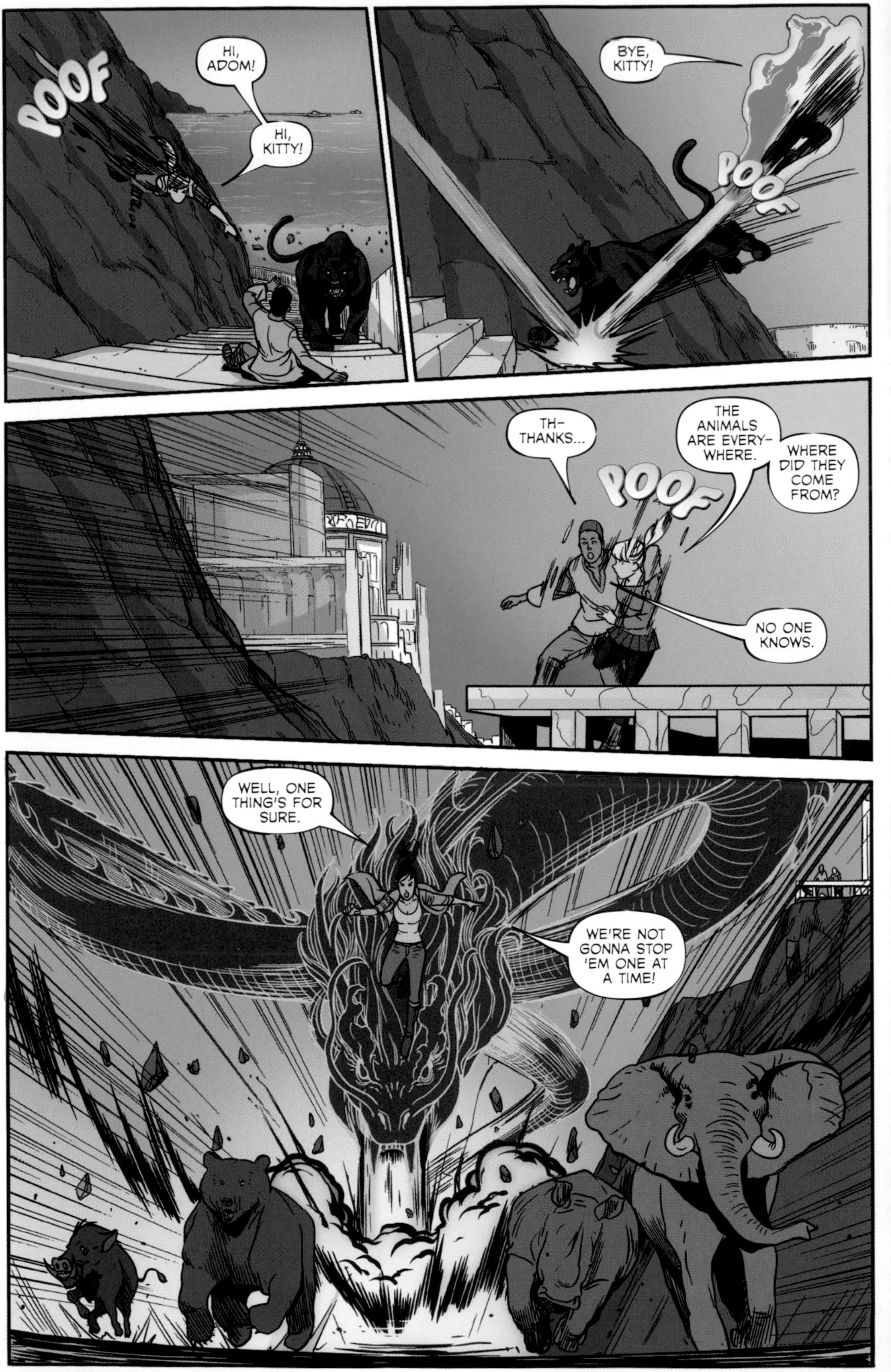
POOF
HI, ADOM!
HI, KITTY!
BYE, KITTY!
POOF
TH-THANKS...
THE ANIMALS ARE EVERY-WHERE.
POOF
WHERE DID THEY COME FROM?
NO ONE KNOWS.
WELL, ONE THING'S FOR SURE.
WE'RE NOT GONNA STOP 'EM ONE AT A TIME!

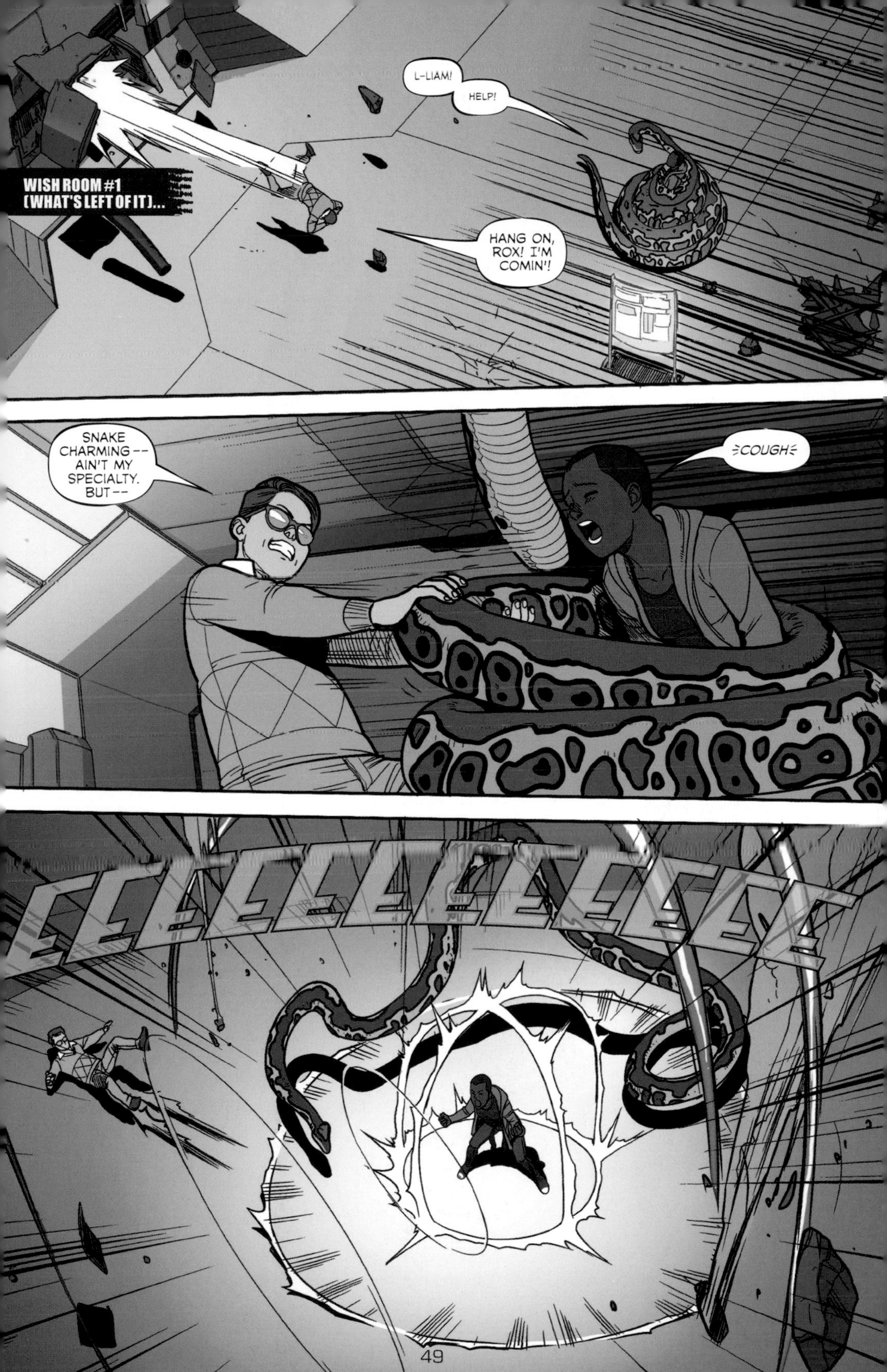
WISH ROOM #1
(WHAT'S LEFT OF IT)...
L-LIAM!
HELP!
HANG ON, ROX! I'M COMIN'!
SNAKE CHARMING -- AIN'T MY SPECIALTY. BUT --
=COUGH=

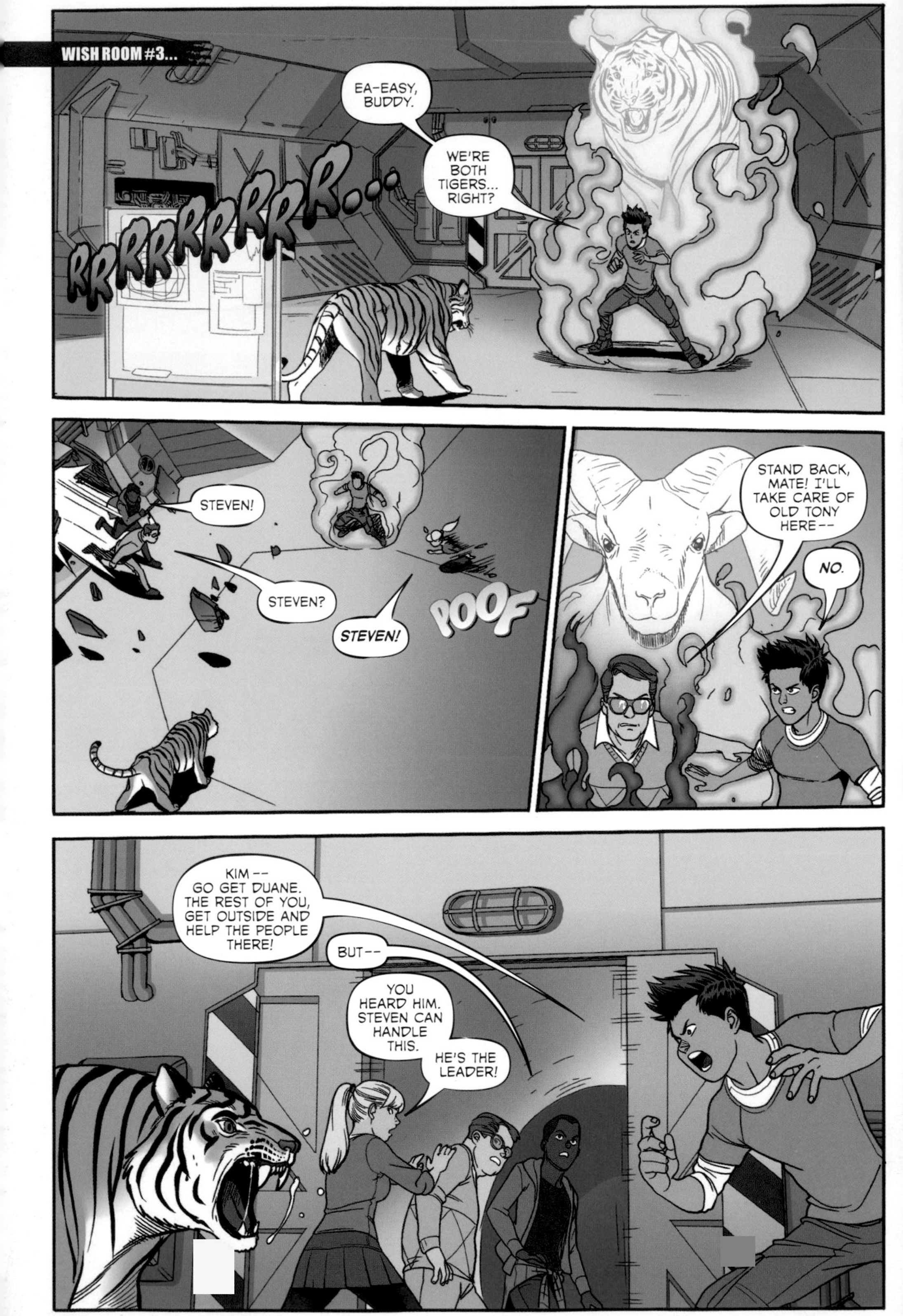
WISH ROOM #3...
EA-EASY, BUDDY.
WE'RE BOTH TIGERS... RIGHT?
RRRRRRRRRR...
STEVEN!
STEVEN?
STEVEN!
POOF
STAND BACK, MATE! I'LL TAKE CARE OF OLD TONY HERE--
NO.
KIM -- GO GET DUANE. THE REST OF YOU, GET OUTSIDE AND HELP THE PEOPLE THERE!
BUT--
YOU HEARD HIM. STEVEN CAN HANDLE THIS.
HE'S THE LEADER!

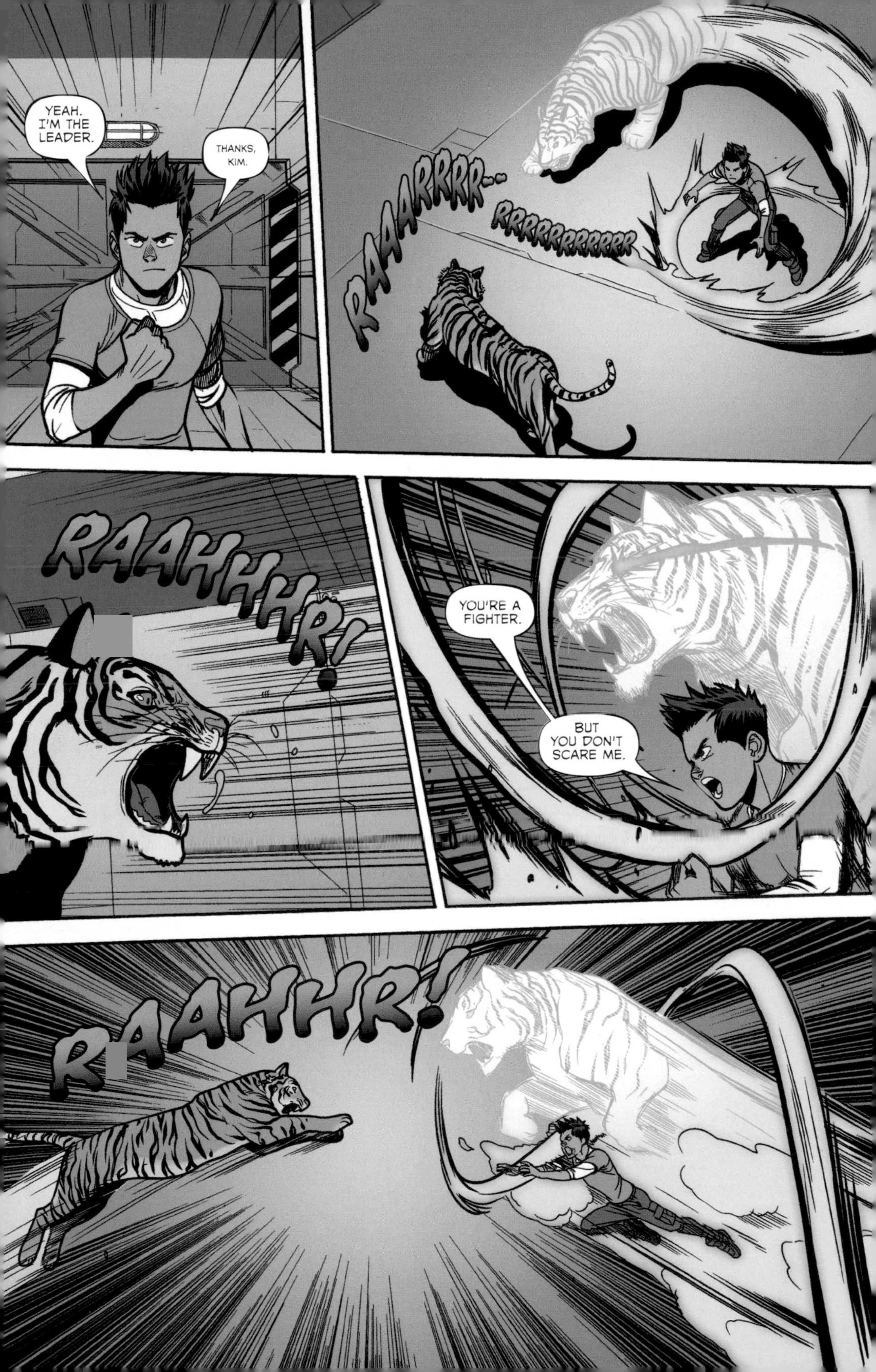
YEAH. I'M THE LEADER.
THANKS, KIM.
RAAARRRR--
RRRRRRRRRRR
RAAHHHR!
YOU'RE A FIGHTER.
BUT YOU DON'T SCARE ME.
RAAHHR!

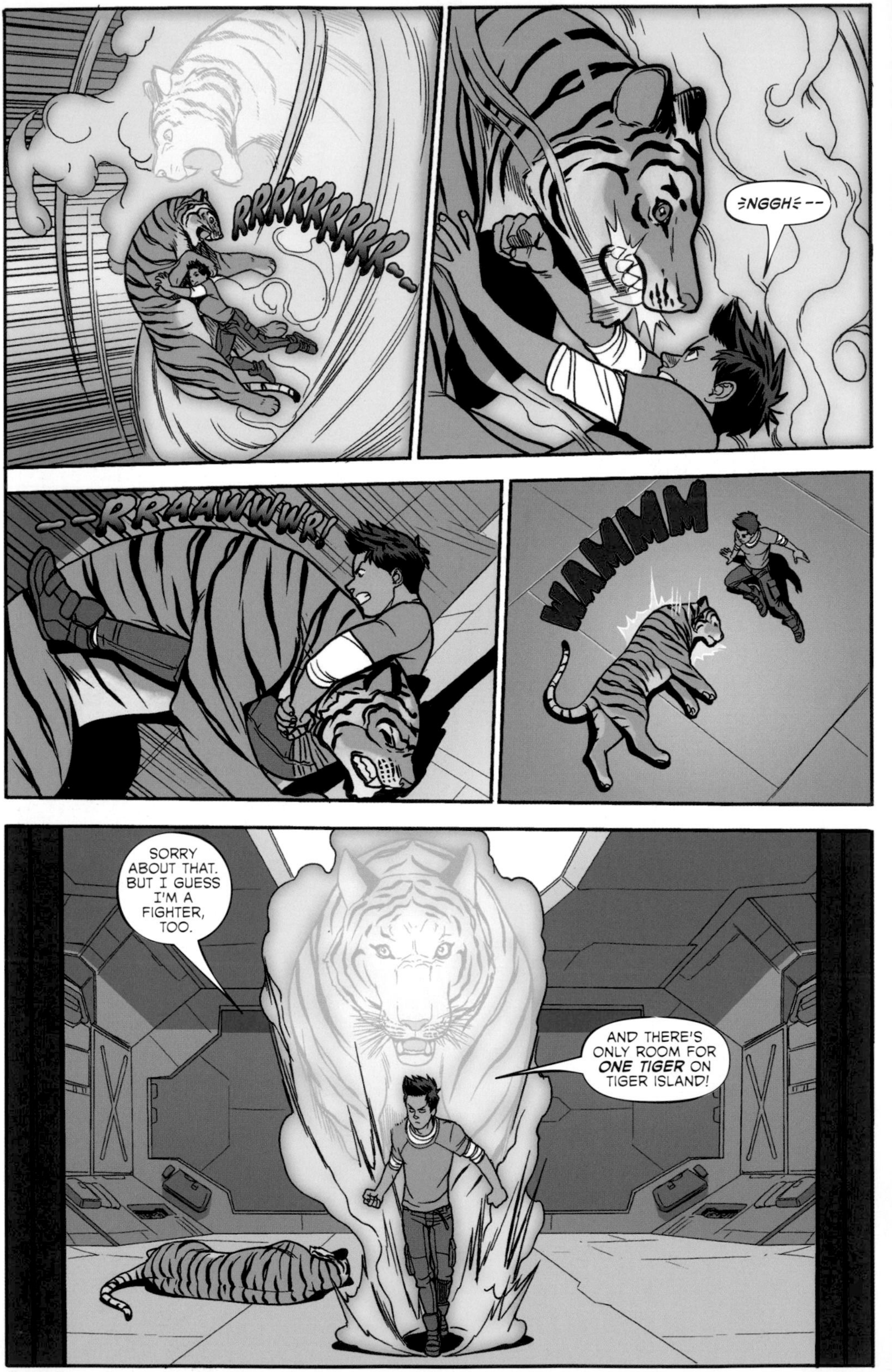
RRRRRRRRRRR--
NGGH--
--RRAAWWWR!
WAMMM
SORRY ABOUT THAT. BUT I GUESS I'M A FIGHTER, TOO.
AND THERE'S ONLY ROOM FOR ***ONE TIGER*** ON TIGER ISLAND!

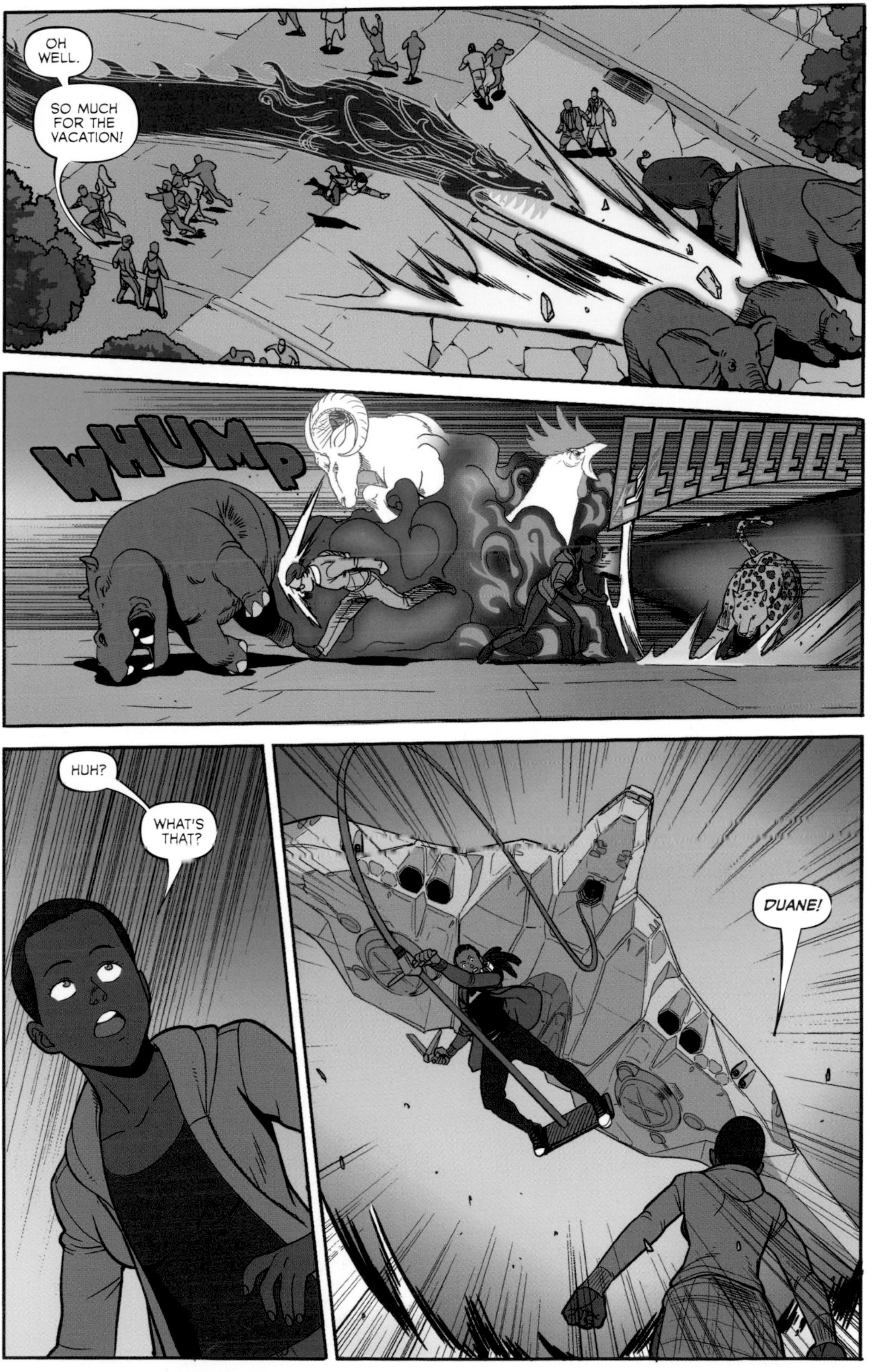
OH WELL.
SO MUCH FOR THE VACATION!
WHUMP
EEEEEEEEE
HUH?
WHAT'S THAT?
DUANE!

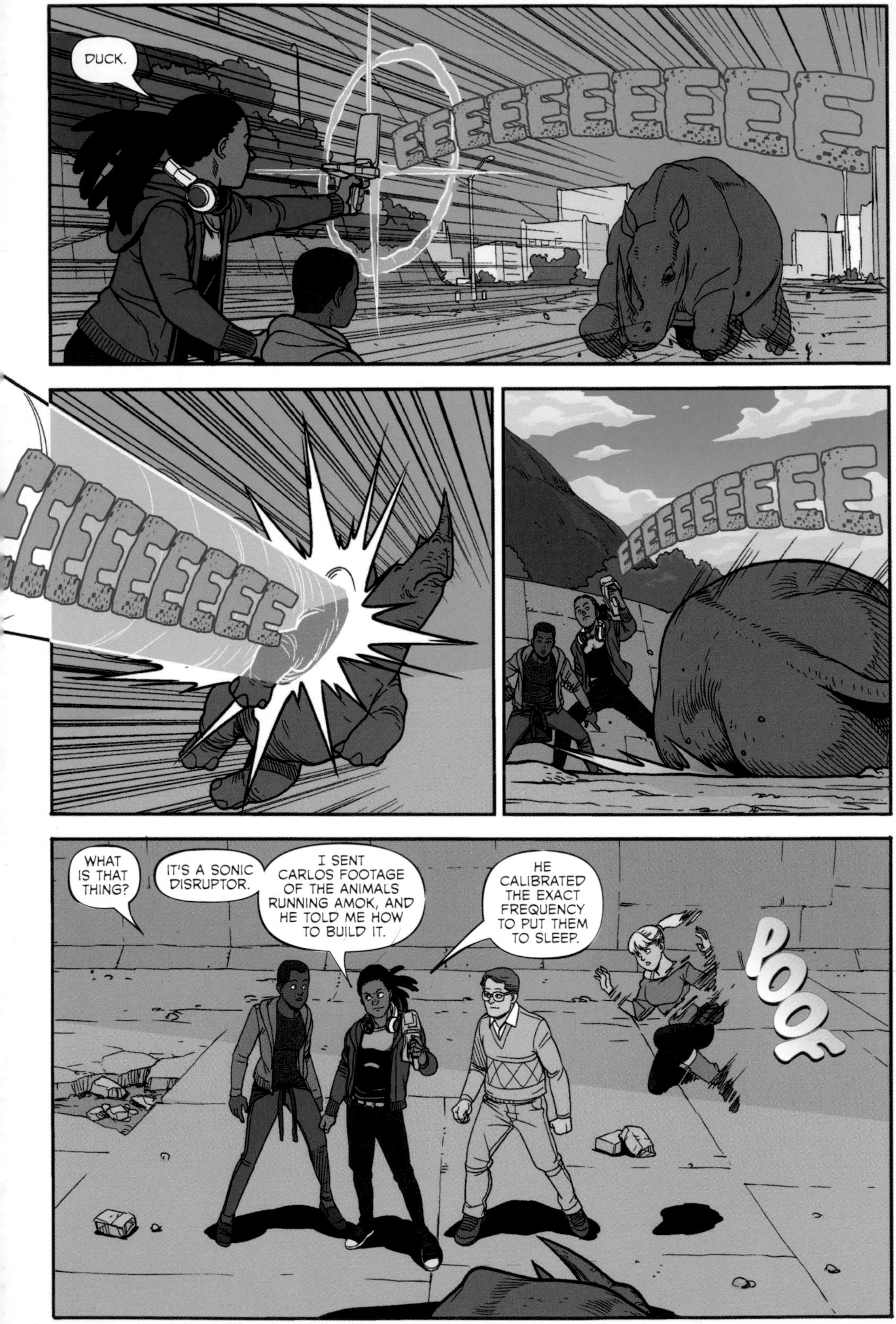
DUCK.
EEEEEEEEEEEE
EEEEEEEEEEE
EEEEEEEEEEEE
WHAT IS THAT THING?
IT'S A SONIC DISRUPTOR.
I SENT CARLOS FOOTAGE OF THE ANIMALS RUNNING AMOK, AND HE TOLD ME HOW TO BUILD IT.
HE CALIBRATED THE EXACT FREQUENCY TO PUT THEM TO SLEEP.
POOF

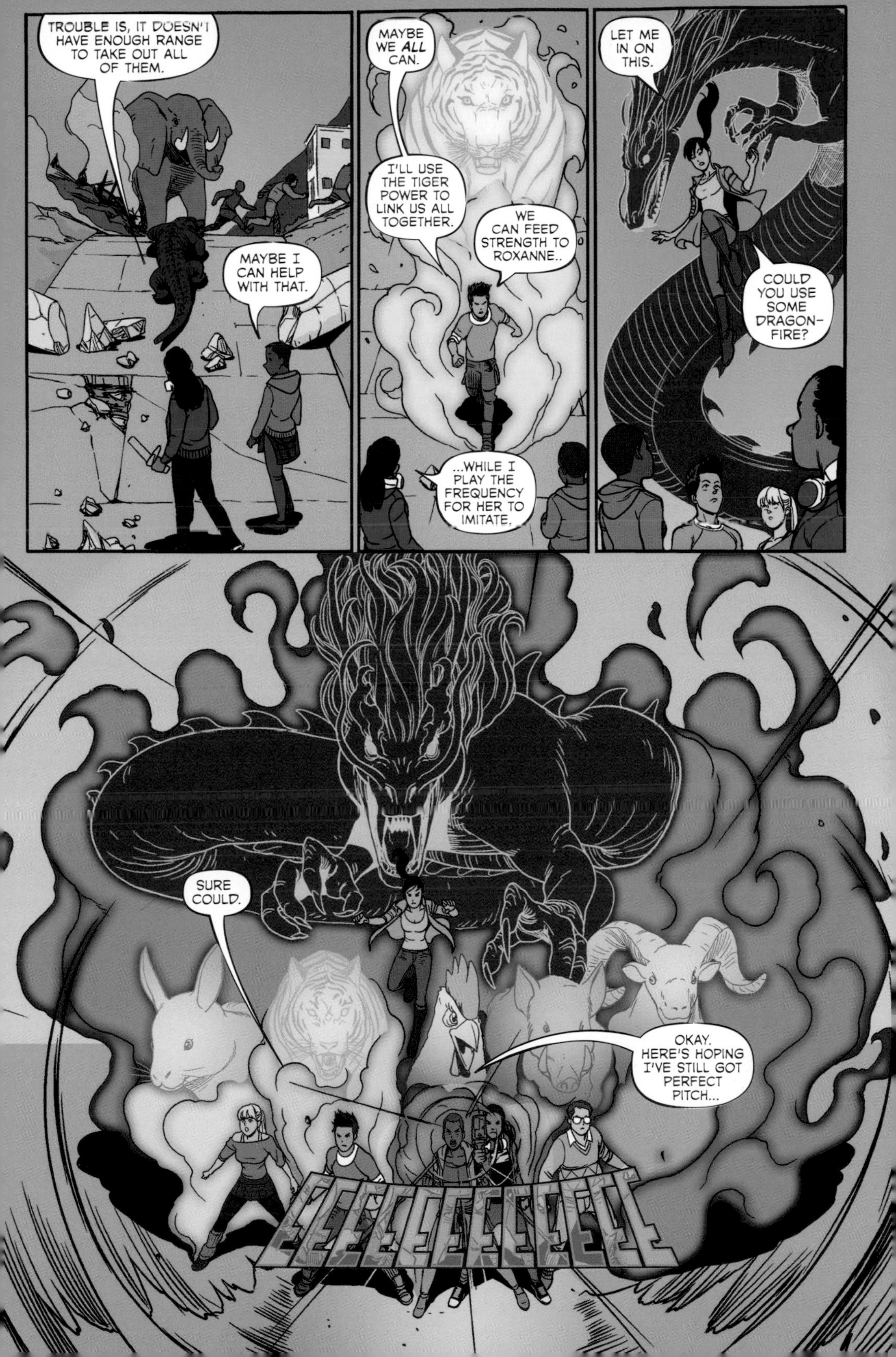
TROUBLE IS, IT DOESN'T HAVE ENOUGH RANGE TO TAKE OUT ALL OF THEM.
MAYBE I CAN HELP WITH THAT.
MAYBE WE *ALL* CAN.
I'LL USE THE TIGER POWER TO LINK US ALL TOGETHER.
WE CAN FEED STRENGTH TO ROXANNE..
...WHILE I PLAY THE FREQUENCY FOR HER TO IMITATE.
LET ME IN ON THIS.
COULD YOU USE SOME DRAGON-FIRE?
SURE COULD.
OKAY. HERE'S HOPING I'VE STILL GOT PERFECT PITCH...
EEEEEEEEEEE

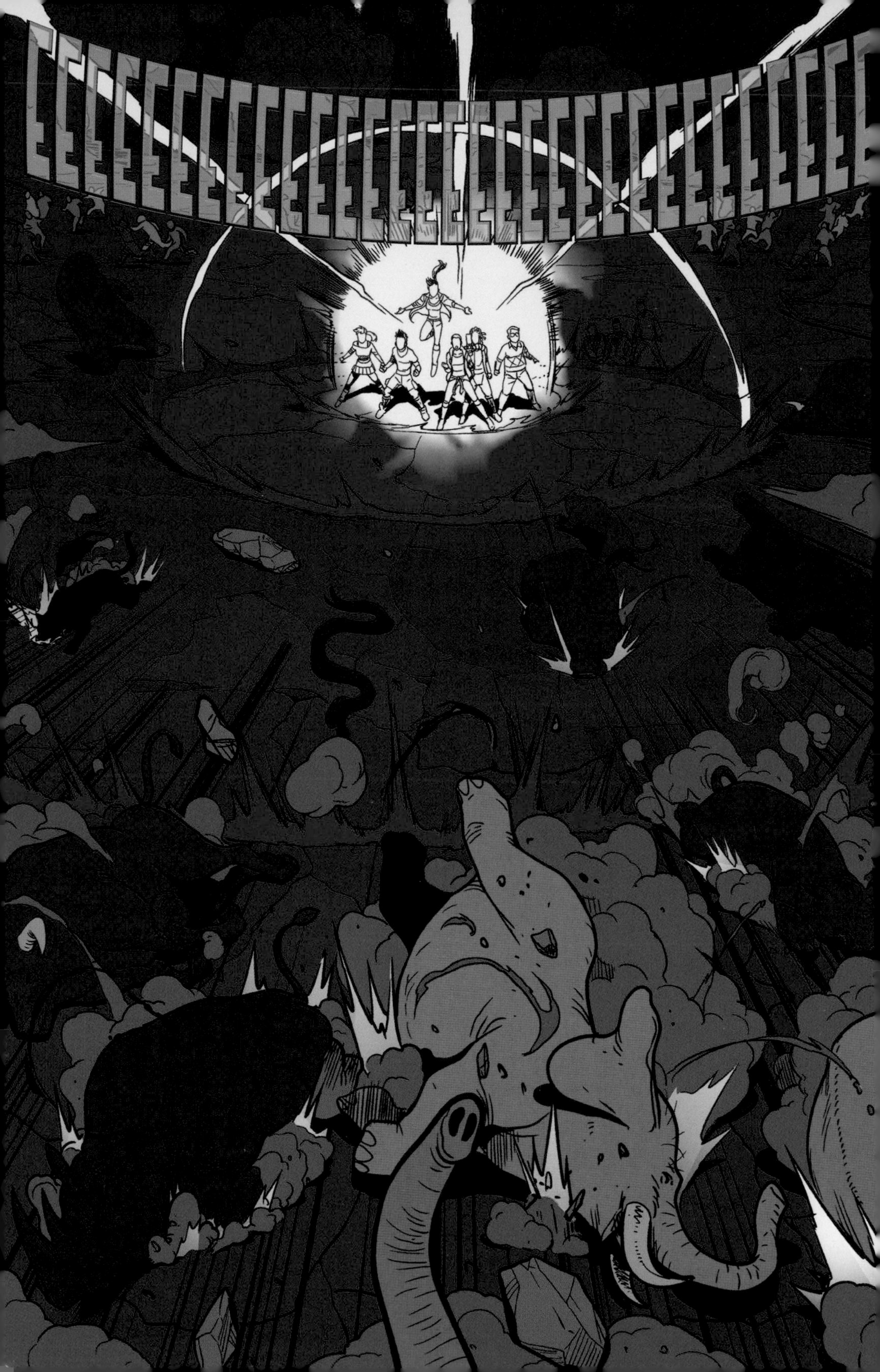
EEEEEEEEEEEEEEEEEEEEEEEEEEEEEEEE

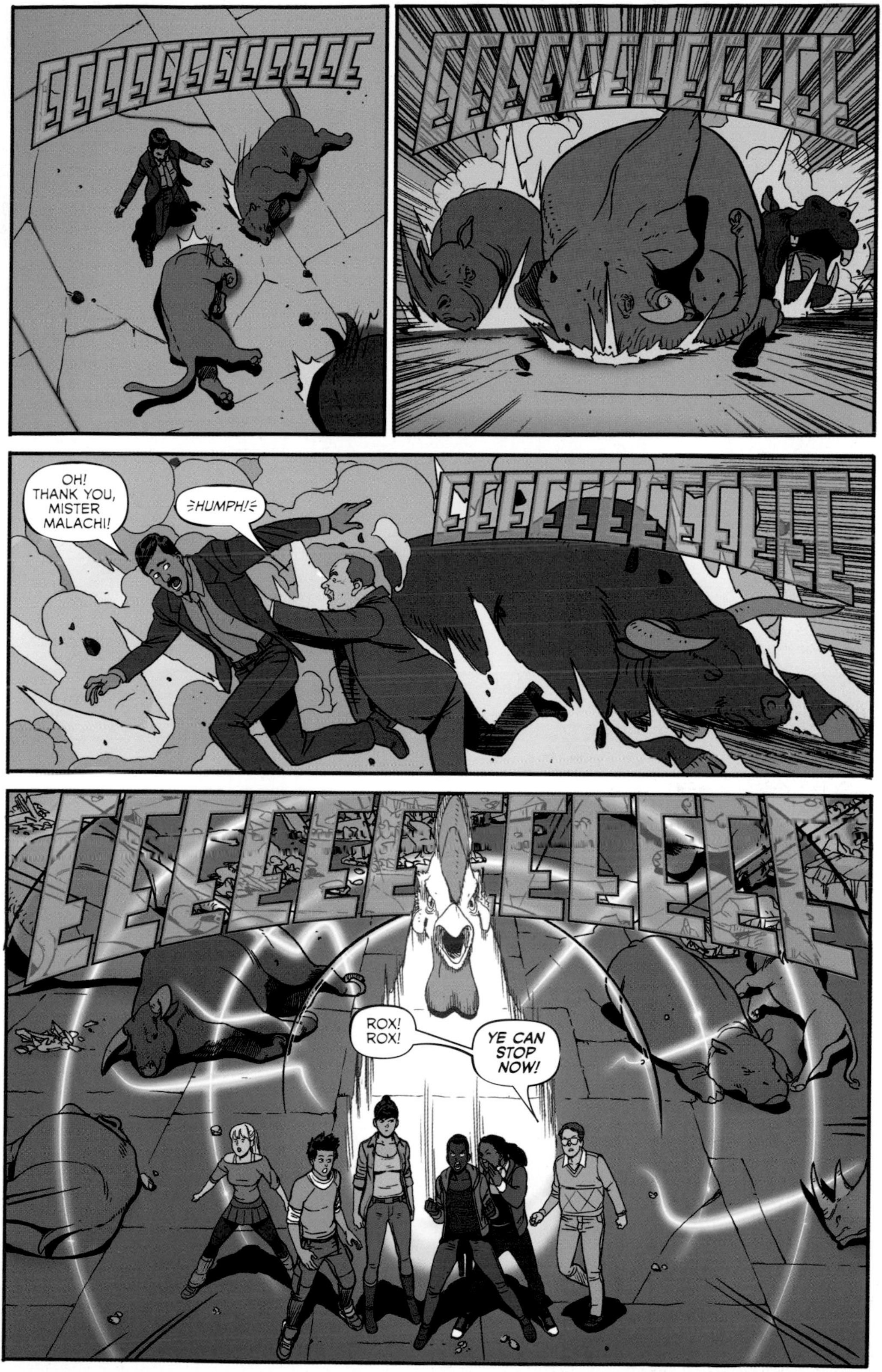
EEEEEEEEEEEE
EEEEEEEEEEE
OH! THANK YOU, MISTER MALACHI!
HUMPH!
EEEEEEEEEEE
EEEEEEEEEEEEE
ROX! ROX!
YE CAN STOP NOW!

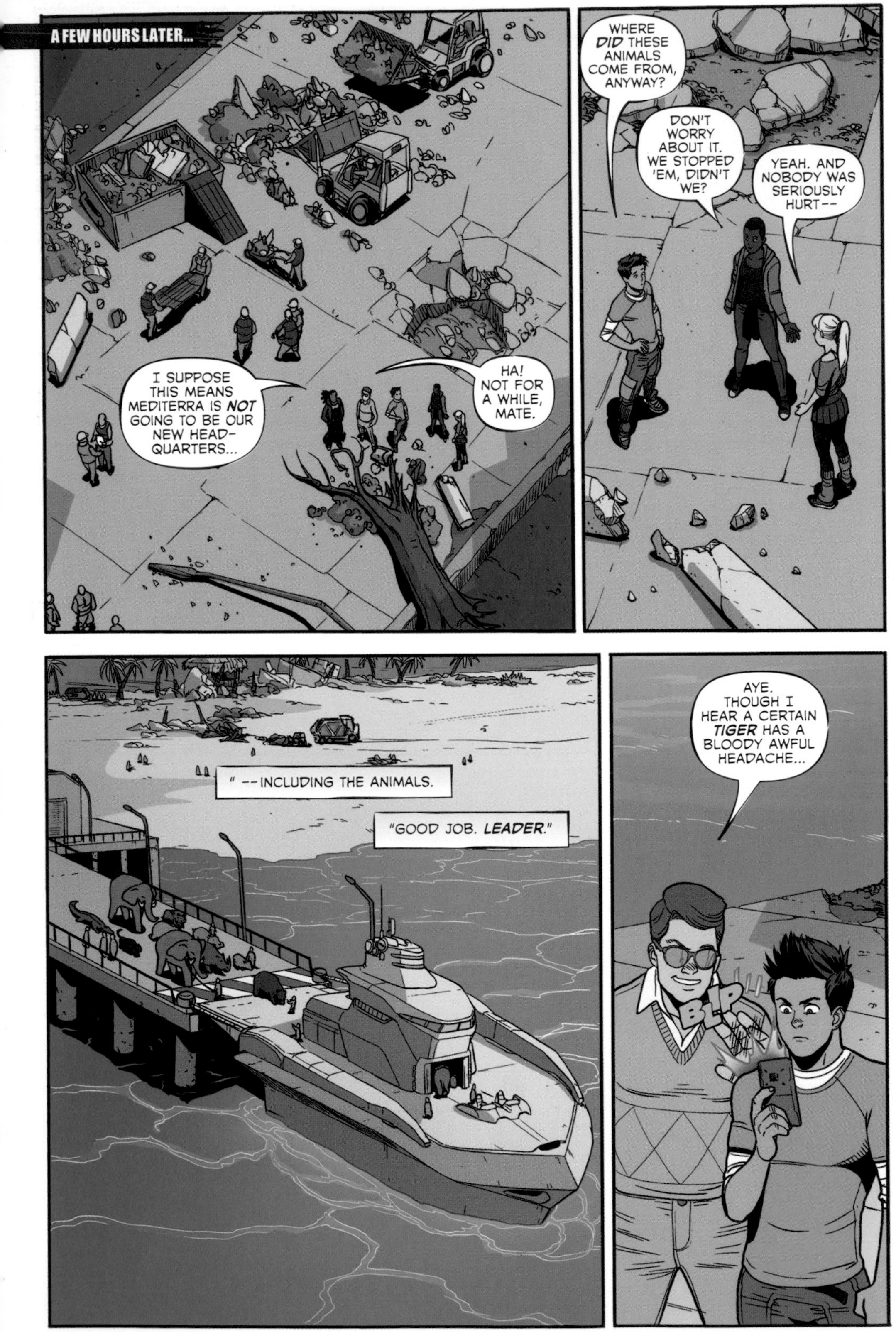
A FEW HOURS LATER...
I SUPPOSE THIS MEANS MEDITERRA IS NOT GOING TO BE OUR NEW HEAD-QUARTERS...
HA! NOT FOR A WHILE, MATE.
WHERE DID THESE ANIMALS COME FROM, ANYWAY?
DON'T WORRY ABOUT IT. WE STOPPED 'EM, DIDN'T WE?
YEAH. AND NOBODY WAS SERIOUSLY HURT--
" --INCLUDING THE ANIMALS.
"GOOD JOB. LEADER."
AYE. THOUGH I HEAR A CERTAIN TIGER HAS A BLOODY AWFUL HEADACHE...
BLIP

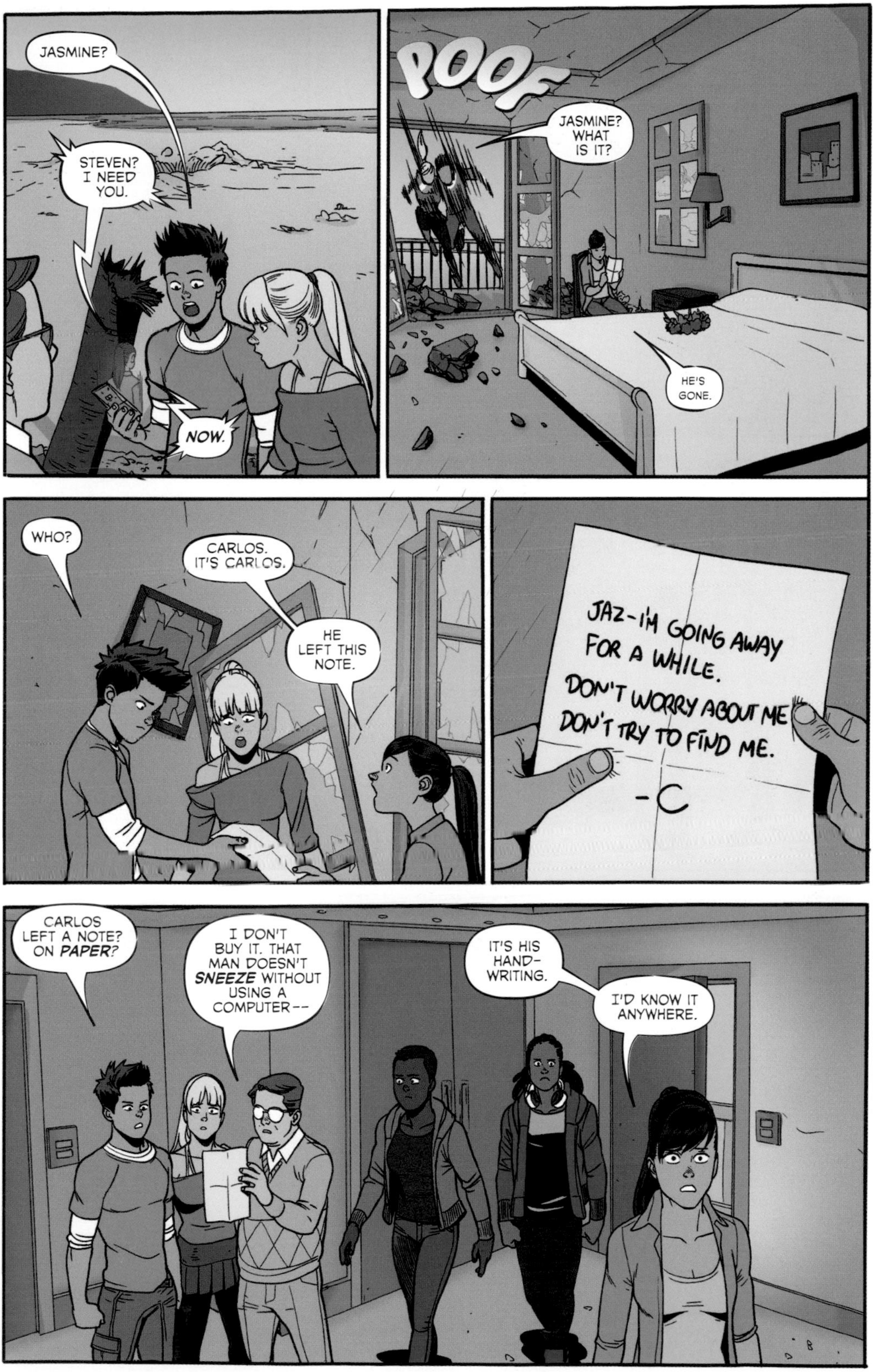
JASMINE?
STEVEN? I NEED YOU.
NOW.
POOF
JASMINE? WHAT IS IT?
HE'S GONE.
WHO?
CARLOS. IT'S CARLOS.
HE LEFT THIS NOTE.
JAZ- I'M GOING AWAY FOR A WHILE.
DON'T WORRY ABOUT ME
DON'T TRY TO FIND ME.
-C
CARLOS LEFT A NOTE? ON *PAPER*?
I DON'T BUY IT. THAT MAN DOESN'T *SNEEZE* WITHOUT USING A COMPUTER--
IT'S HIS HAND-WRITING.
I'D KNOW IT ANYWHERE.

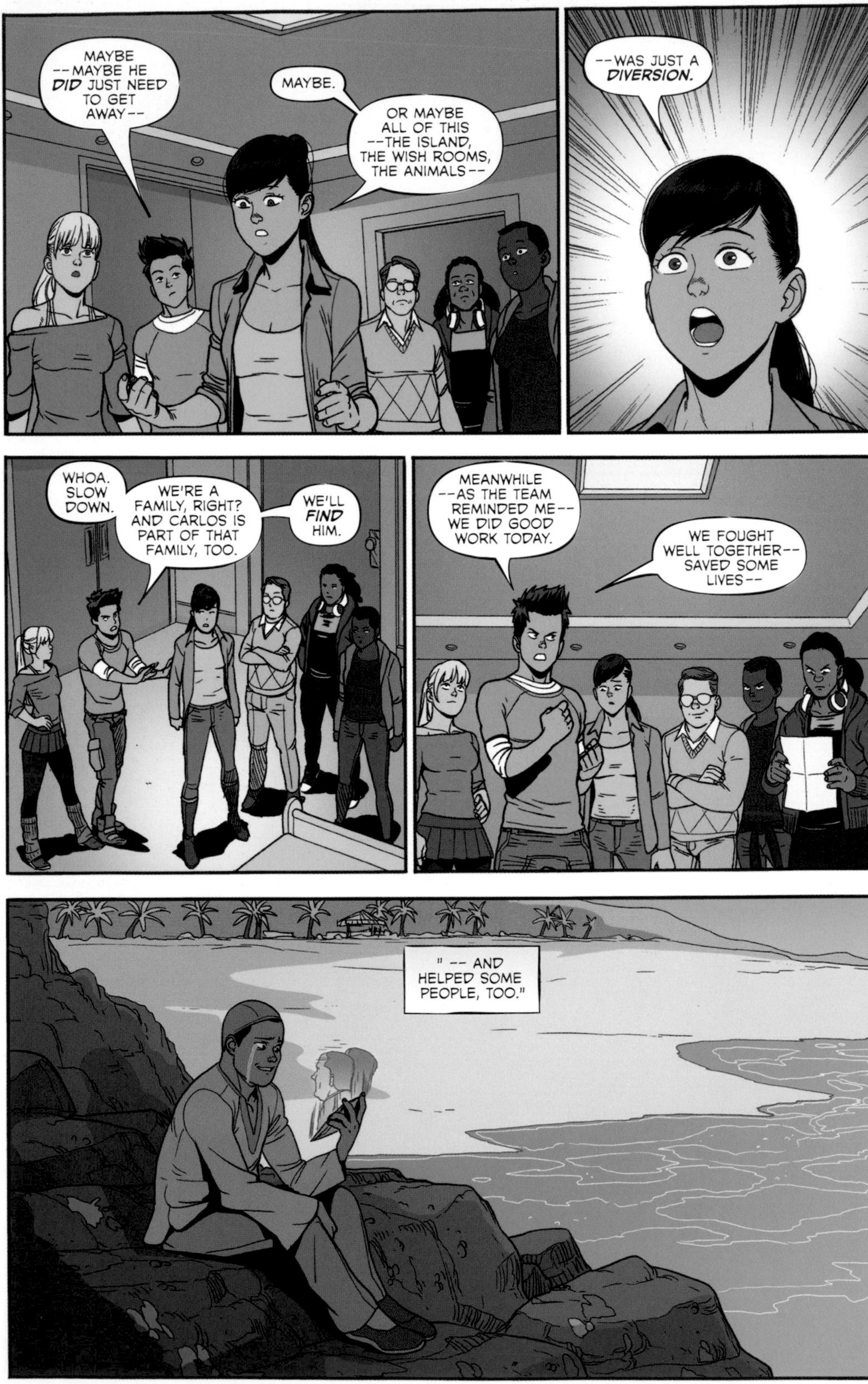
MAYBE --MAYBE HE DID JUST NEED TO GET AWAY--
MAYBE.
OR MAYBE ALL OF THIS --THE ISLAND, THE WISH ROOMS, THE ANIMALS--
--WAS JUST A DIVERSION.
WHOA. SLOW DOWN.
WE'RE A FAMILY, RIGHT? AND CARLOS IS PART OF THAT FAMILY, TOO.
WE'LL FIND HIM.
MEANWHILE --AS THE TEAM REMINDED ME-- WE DID GOOD WORK TODAY.
WE FOUGHT WELL TOGETHER-- SAVED SOME LIVES--
" -- AND HELPED SOME PEOPLE, TOO."

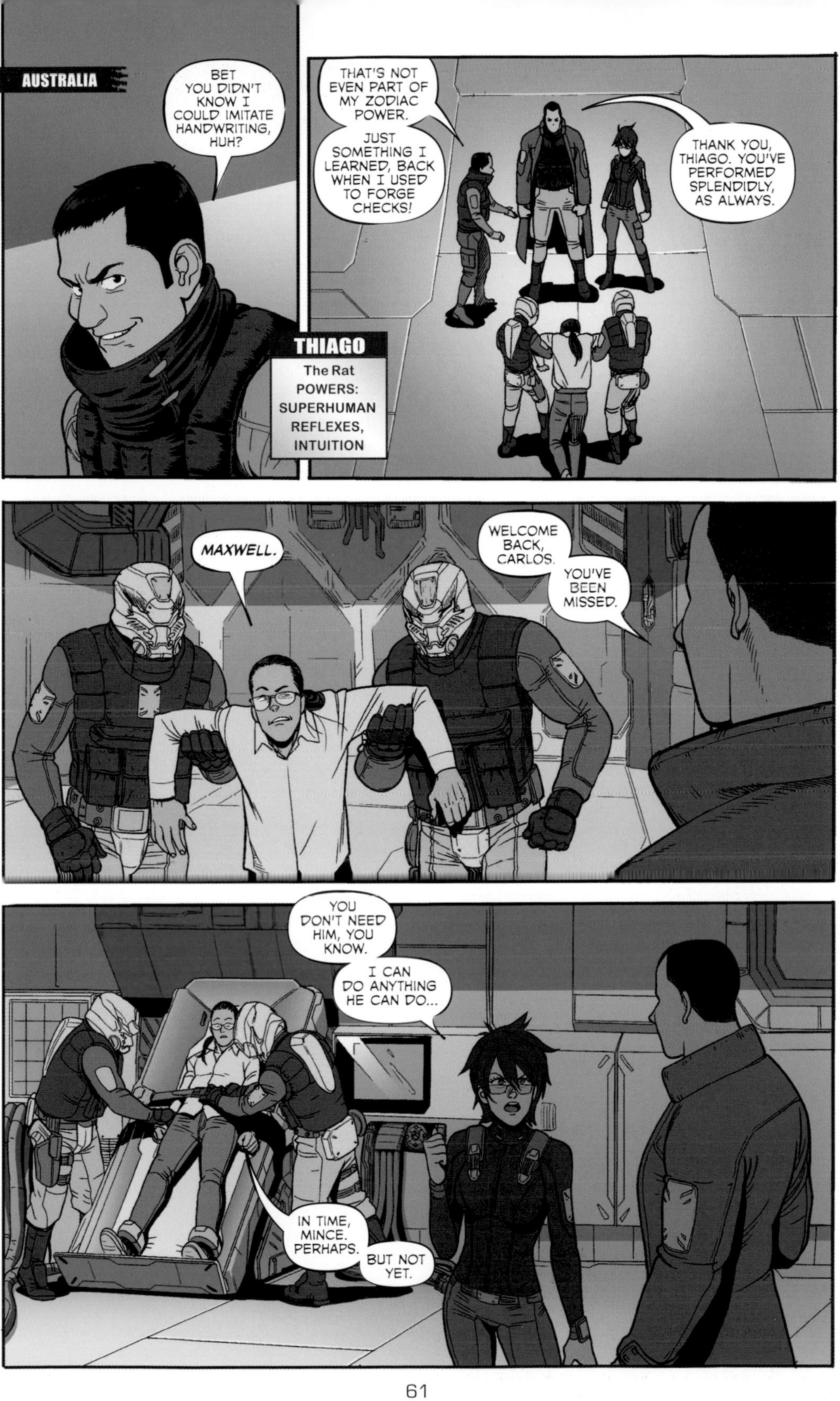
AUSTRALIA
BET YOU DIDN'T KNOW I COULD IMITATE HANDWRITING, HUH?
THIAGO
The Rat
POWERS: SUPERHUMAN REFLEXES, INTUITION
THAT'S NOT EVEN PART OF MY ZODIAC POWER.
JUST SOMETHING I LEARNED, BACK WHEN I USED TO FORGE CHECKS!
THANK YOU, THIAGO. YOU'VE PERFORMED SPLENDIDLY, AS ALWAYS.
MAXWELL.
WELCOME BACK, CARLOS.
YOU'VE BEEN MISSED.
YOU DON'T NEED HIM, YOU KNOW.
I CAN DO ANYTHING HE CAN DO...
IN TIME, MINCE. PERHAPS.
BUT NOT YET.

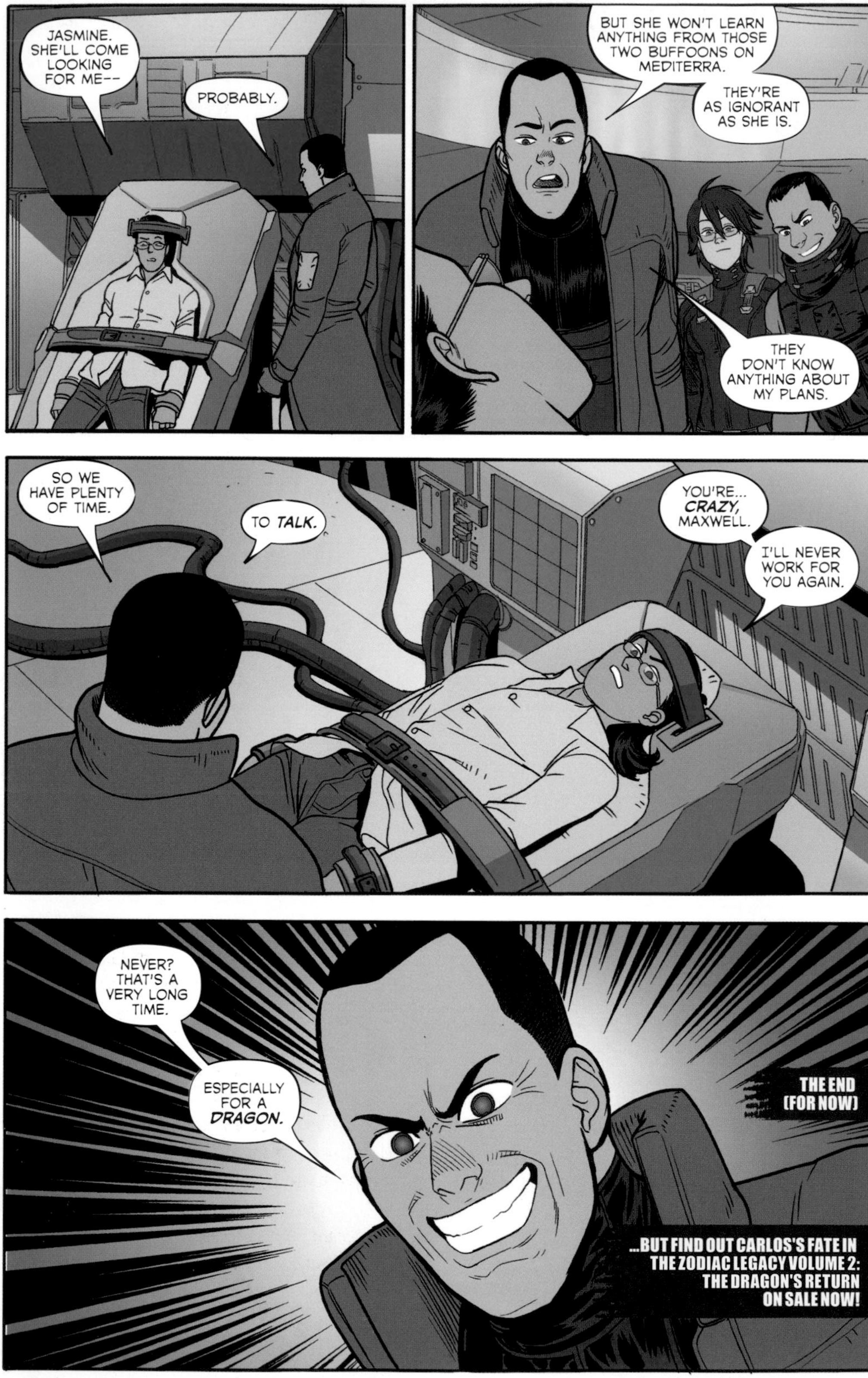
JASMINE. SHE'LL COME LOOKING FOR ME--
PROBABLY.
BUT SHE WON'T LEARN ANYTHING FROM THOSE TWO BUFFOONS ON MEDITERRA.
THEY'RE AS IGNORANT AS SHE IS.
THEY DON'T KNOW ANYTHING ABOUT MY PLANS.
SO WE HAVE PLENTY OF TIME.
TO TALK.
YOU'RE... CRAZY, MAXWELL.
I'LL NEVER WORK FOR YOU AGAIN.
NEVER? THAT'S A VERY LONG TIME.
ESPECIALLY FOR A DRAGON.
THE END (FOR NOW)
...BUT FIND OUT CARLOS'S FATE IN THE ZODIAC LEGACY VOLUME 2: THE DRAGON'S RETURN ON SALE NOW!